Conte

The Wandering Lovers

Far, far away in the midst of a pine forest there once lived one of the most beautiful young men anyone had ever seen. His name was Ladgate, and he lived with his father and mother in a modest house where they made a living as carpenters and keepers of chickens, geese and pigs. They lived not far from the nearest town, a place called Berl, and every week Ladgate would go there with an array of livestock and carpentry to sell, and every week would come back with his pockets bulging from the eager purchases of the women of the town.

'That Ladgate,' the men would say to their wives, 'he certainly has got the gift of the gab. That's the sixth goose he's sold you in as many weeks.'

'Yes,' their wives would agree incredulously, 'that's it, the gift of the gab.'

But Ladgate never paid any mind to his adoring customers, for his mind was on another.

Ladgate and his family didn't live alone in their pine forest. Nearby lived a family of potters. Like Ladgate's there were 3 in this family, a mother, father, and a daughter, by the name of Hatnik. Hatnik was the same age as Ladgate, and like him was immeasurably beautiful. Unlike Ladgate, however, she wouldn't venture into town to sell her wares, but stayed in the house making the finest pots that her parents would take into the town to sell. Few had ever seen Hatnik, but those that had had fallen instantly in love with her.

Ladgate and Hatnik had known each other since childhood, and had grown up playing together in the forest. As they had grown their friendship had turned into love, and they had never had eyes for anyone else. They would snatch any opportunity they could to be together, and both assumed that when the time came they would marry each other, which is why Hatnik was so surprised when her parents turned to her one morning over breakfast and said,

'Are you looking forward to marrying the duke?'

Hatnik had to confess that she wasn't, for not only was she not marrying the duke, but she had never even met the man.

'Oh, but you are,' her mother said to her patiently, 'you didn't think we'd let you marry a carpenter's son did you?'

Hatnik had rather thought her parents would.

'Don't be silly,' said her father. 'Someone with your looks? That would never do. No, the duke has heard of your staggering beauty and has expressed a desire to marry you. We have expressed a desire for you to marry the duke and so the matter is settled. The wedding is next week.'

Hatnik's parents were not cruel, they simply wanted the best for their daughter, and to their minds her marrying a duke as opposed to the lowly son of a carpenter was much better for her. It was a way of thinking that was shared by Ladgate's parents,

'Don't think you'll be marrying that potter girl next door,' they said to him that very same night. 'She's not nearly good enough for you.'

'But I love her,' Ladgate countered.

'No no,' Ladgate's mother told him. 'You can do much better than that. Aim higher, an aristocrat or someone like that is what you should be going for with your looks.'

'But I don't want an aristocrat,' Ladgate protested, 'I want Hatnik.'

'I'm afraid you can't have her,' his father told him. 'We're marrying you up, not sideways.'

Distraught, the two lovers met that night in secret to discuss their situation. Hatnik had already packed her bag, having decided that that only thing to be done was to elope. Ladgate wasn't so sure.

'But what about my parents?' he asked. 'They'll be furious!'

Hatnick looked at him blankly,

'Don't you love me?' she asked.

'Of course I do,' said Ladgate. 'But they don't think you're good enough.'

Hatnik was unimpressed.

'Who cares? Mine don't think you're good enough. That doesn't matter.'

'But we can't just run off,' Ladgate said miserably, staring at his feet 'because….'

But he trailed off as he looked up and realised that the half sentence he had begun had been the most stupid thing he had ever said in his life. Not waiting to hear any more, Hatnik had picked up her bag and disappeared into the night.

There was no sign of her the next day. Nor the next, nor the one after that. As the days turned into weeks it became clear to everyone that she wasn't coming back. After a month the duke cancelled the wedding. Still Hatnik didn't return. The months turned into years without any sign of Hatnik. Life returned to normal for everyone except Ladgate, who remained as miserable and heartbroken as he had been the night when she had left him forever.

One day a beautiful young woman came to Berl. She was dressed in fine clothes and had pockets full of money. No one knew where she came from or what she did, but everyone agreed that whatever it was she must be good at it for she was fabulously wealthy. She stayed in the local inn, and seemed to be in urgent need of furniture, for she asked all she met if there might be a carpenter in the town, perhaps living in a pine forest nearby.

There was indeed, she was told, but she wouldn't get anything from him for a while, he was too busy preparing for his son's wedding.

At this the lady let out an involuntary cry.

Oh yes. Hadn't she heard? The carpenter had a son who was the most beautiful man anyone had ever seen. His face, they said, brought gods to their knees. His smile could launch a thousand ships, and his perfect frame made the most flawless sunset purple with jealousy. His famed beauty had even reached the ears of the princess, and she had travelled halfway across the kingdom to demand that he marry her.

Demand?

Like all that's beautiful, the carpenter's son was voiceless, she was told. He had been for many years now. No one knew why, but one day he had simply stopped talking, and gone around with a visage as sad and lonely as anyone you could ever meet. Anyone would think he had lost his true love.

At this the lady permitted herself a slight smile.

There was never any question of his accepting the princess' hand in marriage - what the princess wanted the princess got, and so she and the carpenter's son were to be married a week from that very day. They were at the palace at that moment, both of them, preparing for the big event.

At this the lady's gorgeous eyes blazed, and one of her lovely hands darted into a pocket and emerged with a bag full of gold coins which she flung onto the table in front of her.

'I need the fastest horse you can spare, and directions to the royal palace.'

When she got to the palace, Hatnik (for is was she) tied her horse to a tree safely out of sight and approached the gates, summoning her most spectacular smile.

'I'm one of the dancers here for the royal wedding, might I be allowed in?'

The guards never stood a chance.

Once she was in the palace it was a bit trickier, but Hatnik had spent most of her life being seen and not heard, and seeing as she looked every inch the beautiful aristocrat she found that she had no trouble in gliding from room to room, her eyes silently hunting for her beloved while her smile disarmed all. She eventually saw him, listening mournfully as a footman lectured him on the correct way to dress for dinner, looking every inch as gorgeous as she remembered. She took care that he didn't see her, but as he left and set off on his own down a corridor back to his room she accosted him.

To say that he was shocked was an understatement. To say that he was happy is to do happiness a disservice. He had dreamt about this moment a thousand times a day since Hatnik had left, rehearsing it over and over in the mirror, never quite managing to get right what he wanted to say. In the event, he said, as he found his voice for the first time in years, simply,

'I still love you.'

Hatnik frowned at him.

'Is that the best you can do?'

Ladgate had to admit that it wasn't the best line, but it was true.

'I'm sorry. Not a day goes by when I don't regret letting you go that night. I....I.....Please forgive me,' he finished lamely.

'Don't marry the princess,' said Hatnik.

Ladgate sighed.

'What the princess wants the princess gets. My darling, there will never be room for anyone in my heart but you, but if I were to call off the marriage the princess would kill me. She doesn't take kindly to being thwarted.'

'What if –' Hatnik began, but Ladgate had already seen the princess approaching from the other end of the corridor.

'I have to go now, my love, I'm sorry,' was all he could manage before the princess had him in her arms and Hatnik had melted away before anyone was any the wiser.

That night, back at the inn, Hatnik was not in the best of moods. She must stop that marriage, but how? She wasn't a swashbuckling pirate with a band of merry men, or a big strong giant who could simply knock out all the guards and carry her love away. She had no skills of any sort. What could she do?

One of her flawless hands went to her money pouch. She needed another drink. Only her money pouch wasn't there. Confused, she patted her other pocket. It wasn't there either. She was just starting to get alarmed when she saw a tall, slender man all in black paying for two drinks at the bar. He was a strange enough fellow to look at to be sure, but what really interested her was the fact that he was paying with her money pouch. Indignant, she stood up and watched as the man took the two drinks over to a table where another man sat. Well, she assumed it was a man, but he was so small that she would have been forgiven for mistaking him for a child, or even a doll. He was sitting on the table, not at it, for if he had sitting on a stool he would have been quite lost to his friend sitting at the table opposite him. He has barely bigger than the flagon of beer that he was presented with, and it was with fascination that Hatnik watched him stand and manage to lift and drink from a vessel that was the same size as him. He must be tremendously strong, she thought as she approached the pair with her knife drawn.

'You have my money pouch,' she said to the tall man as she held her knife against his throat.

The little man let out a small squeak. The tall man put down his beer.

'Aha!' he said. 'At last, she notices us!'

And he tossed her money pouch back to her.

'I'm very grateful for the beer. Please sit down and join us.'

Hatnik sat down and joined them.

'If you wanted to get my attention you could have just said hello, you know.'

The tall man shrugged, and Hatnik noticed that he was wearing one of her rings.

'What?'

The tall man shrugged again and tossed the ring back to her.

'My name is Nabo, I am a master thief. This here is Kov, he is the smallest man alive.'

The little man bowed. Nabo continued.

'We have been watching you for some time now.'

'Why?'

'You are beautiful, new to town, you have been asking lots of questions, and today you visited the palace. How could I not be intrigued? And ever since you have come back from the palace today you have looked more depressed than a man who has had his boots stolen on the eve of a boot throwing competition,' Nabo looked at her, suddenly serious. 'And believe me, madam, I know what that looks like. Tell us, what is the matter? Perhaps we can help.'

'Why would you help me?' Hatnik asked, not unreasonably.

'Because life isn't fair and it never will be,' Nabo told her. 'But that doesn't mean that we shouldn't try to make it so.'

Quite rightly dismissing this as the rubbish that it was, Hatnik nevertheless found herself telling the two men all about Ladgate, and his unfortunate impending marriage to the princess.

'But how can I stop the marriage?'

At this Nabo became very excited and jumped to his feet. So did Kov, but he was so small that no one noticed.

'We shall steal him away!'

Hatnik was still not convinced.

'What's in it for you?'

'In truth,' Nabo told her, 'I have always felt that it should be I who marry the princess. I have been dealt such a poor hand in life I think that it is the least I deserve.'

His little companion nodded in sympathy.

'I don't think you've thought this through,' said Hatnik. 'Why do you think that just because you steal the princess's potential husband from her she will agree to marry you?

'It is simple,' Nabo told her.

He was holding her bracelet now and playing with it. She hadn't even noticed it leave her wrist.

'I will steal her heart.'

Even for a master thief, Hatnik doubted that this was possible. Still, if these two could help her to steal Ladgate then it wasn't of much concern of hers what happened afterwards.

'Very well,' she said, 'if we do this, I get Ladgate and you get the princess, but what' she asked, pointing at little Kov, 'do you get?'

Kov jumped up and down excitedly and made a little squeaking noise.

'He has no doubt that there is plenty of cheese at the palace,' Nabo explained. 'He loves cheese.'

And so it was settled. Over the next few days Nabo and Kov planned and schemed and spied while Hatnik bought them drinks, until by the night before the wedding they had it all worked out.

That night they rode to the high palace walls under cover of darkness. Nabo produced a rope from his pocket that he tied around Kov's waist. He then tossed the little man high over the wall into the palace gardens.

Hatnik looked at Nabo as Kov sailed up into the darkness.

'Won't he hurt himself when he lands?

The thief shrugged.

'We do it all the time, madam.'

Once in the garden, Kov tied the rope around a tree and Nabo and Hatnik climbed over. Kov then led them to a locked kitchen door, and Hatnik watched in confusion as the little man set about very quietly tapping all the way around its base. This went on for some time, and she was just about to ask him what he was doing when he made a little squeak of triumph and kicked at the area he was tapping. He had found a small rotten hole, and his foot went right through. He was able to make the hole wider and wider, eventually wide enough for him, to squeeze through into the darkness on the other side.

Nabo turned to Hatnik, seeing her amazement.

'All matter decays, madam. Even love.'

And with that the door clicked open from the inside and Nabo stepped through into the shadows within.

'But love isn't matter,' Hatnik said as she followed him, confused.

But he must not have heard her properly, for as he skipped ahead of her with Kov, the thief said over his shoulder,

'Oh, but it does, madam, love matters more than anything else.'

And with that he became lost in the darkness, and Hatnik had no idea where he had gone.

She stood quite still, trying to get her bearings, but she couldn't even hear the others ahead of her now. She couldn't remember the plan either. She was completely lost. Hatnik was just beginning to panic when she heard a great commotion ahead of her.

At least two people were running in her direction, and the princess, wherever she was, sounded very upset indeed.

The footsteps were upon her now, and suddenly her beloved appeared from the darkness, being pushed roughly by Nabo.

'Quick!' Nabo yelled at them. 'Take two horses from the stables and ride for all you are worth!'

The lovers didn't need to be told twice. They ran to the stables, jumped onto two of the princess' horses, as swift and strong as the wind, and rode straight through the gates, scattering the startled guards. The princess' furious cries followed them out into the night.

Returning to her room the princess was beside herself. How dare they steal her beautiful husband to be! She slammed the door shut in a rage, too angry even to be startled by the tall, thin man lying on her bed.

'Hello, madam,' he drawled seductively.

Even with those two words the princess knew that he had her heart in his hands. And she hadn't even felt him take it.

Ladgate and Hatnik rode through the night, never stopping once for breath. They didn't speak, but were content to bathe in each others' company. They had never been happier. Eventually Ladgate turned to his darling Hatnik.

'She will never stop hunting us, you know. What the princess wants the princess gets.'

Hatnik's face fell.

'But Nabo will steal her heart, won't she stop hunting us then?'

Ladgate shook his head. His wonderful silky hair shone in the moonlight.

'She may not want me anymore, but she will still want revenge.'

'Then we must run forever?'

Ladgate shrugged a perfectly formed shoulder.

'Everybody runs. But not everyone finds someone to run with.'

And the two lovers have never stopped running, for the princess has never stopped hunting for them, no matter how much her new husband pleads with her not to. Theirs is not a happy life, forever looking over their shoulders, often taking it in turns to sleep while the other keeps watch, and always moving from town to town to town. But they have each other. Life isn't fair, but it's better than the alternative.

The Coward and the Troll

There was once a lonely man in a lonely town in the middle of just outside of nowhere who didn't do very much at all. He wasn't very tall, or very handsome, not very good at reading or writing or doing anything useful, and he wasn't very brave. He was, however, a good man. He lived in a town called Megalise, that sat in the middle of a vast, barren plain. It was a town full of outlaws and dishonest folk, and not somewhere that anyone ever went to through choice. In the whole place he was the only good man there was.

But this man, whose name was Coop, was happy enough with his lot in life, and put his total lack of spectacularness in any way down to the hand that life had dealt him rather than anything he might do to change it. Existence, on the whole, was dull for Coop. It wasn't a situation that he liked particularly, but then he never felt sufficiently moved to do anything about it either.

Outside of Megalise lay great danger. The plains beyond its walls were full of bloodthirsty trolls who would have liked nothing more than to eat up every last person who lived there. But the trolls that lived in the Great Plains, like Coop, were great cowards. The townsfolk had found long ago that if they kept up a vigilant guard along the town walls, and threw spears and shouted at any troll that came near then they would be quite safe. Unfortunately the same couldn't be said for anyone to be foolish enough to be caught in the plains after dark, for it was then, away from the town, that the trolls became bold.

And so Coop lived in a kind of an island. The outside world was a scary place, and somewhere that he'd never been to and didn't really think about. He was sure there were things out there, beyond the bone crunching trolls in the Great Plains, but they didn't really hold that much interest for him if he was honest. For Coop, the outside world was a place that he would never visit, and he was equally as sure that nothing from there would ever come to visit him.

All of that changed when one day a beautiful woman arrived without warning in Megalise. She had come, she said, from many miles away, far beyond the Great Plains, and she caused quite a stir in Coop's little island. Where she had come from no one knew.

The town of Megalise was aflame with talk of this beautiful stranger from the moment she arrived. She was all anyone talked or thought of, and Coop was no different to anyone else. Despite this, she and Coop didn't meet until she had been in town for nearly a month. They came across each other one night in the local tavern. As usual a fight had broken out, and there were fists and chairs flying everywhere. Coop saw that this young woman was in danger, and just before a table that had been flung through the air hit her he threw himself in its path, shielding her from harm as the table bounced off his back.

She looked up at him in gratitude.

'I've been staying in this town for some time now,' she said, 'and I haven't met anyone else who would have done something like that for me. Tell me, what's your name?'

'I'm Coop,' Coop said, rubbing his back.

He had only done was what had come naturally; he hadn't been trying to impress the woman.

'And I'm Belle,' she said. 'It's very nice to meet you.'

And so began a friendship that quickly blossomed into love. Like Coop, Belle was kind and thoughtful, and on top of her beauty Coop found this to be irresistible. And Belle was struck by the goodness in Coop, so different to the other men in the town.

This was how, for the first time in his life, Coop found real happiness. Others might have thought Belle's sudden arrival odd, but Coop was not a man to question things, still less to look a gift horse in the mouth. If he had had any thoughts on where Belle might have come from he kept them to himself, and she certainly never talked about her mysterious past.

But curious or no, Coop would have been very surprised to see Belle stealing from the town on a horse late one night and riding stealthily across the vast plains to an old cave many miles away.

She tied her horse to a dead tree outside and went in. After a short distance the cave opened up into a large cavern, in the middle of which flickered a damp fire, casting ghoulish shapes on the wall. Warming himself by this fire sat a troll. He stood up in surprise as his step daughter entered.

'Where have you been?' he roared at her, and struck her with one of his spade like hands, knocking her to the ground.

'Please,' Belle shouted back, holding her face. 'I have come to beg a favour from you.'

'You ran away from me. Why should I do you any favours?' the troll growled.

'I know you've followed me here to the town of Megalise,' Belle told him. `but I've met a man there who I intend to marry. I beg of you, step father, leave this town alone. Please, let it be, and I will do anything you ask.'

'Who is this man?' the troll roared. 'This man who has taken my step daughter from me! I will bite off his head!'

'No!' she cried back angrily, pulling away from him. 'You've raised me and kept me from harm, and I'm grateful, but you cannot rule me forever. Please, let me live in peace in this town, I have repaid my debt to you many times over already.'

'A debt to a troll is never repaid,' the troll told her. 'Who is this man who is taking you away?'

'If you're going to hurt him,' Belle retorted, 'I won't tell you. I love him.'

The troll grabbed Belle by the throat.

'Tell me who he is,' he growled at her.

Belle shook her head defiantly.

The troll squeezed, Belle's face turned purple.

'Tell me,' he said to her, 'for I will not stop squeezing.'

Belle kicked and struggled and tried to scream but it was not use. She couldn't breathe, let alone scream. Eventually it became too much and she signalled to him that she would speak.

'His name's Coop,' she wheezed, 'please don't hurt him!'

But it was too late. The troll had already dropped her and was running for the town in the breaking morning.

Belle was right to be scared. Her step father was not like other trolls; he was no coward. He was fierce and cruel, and Belle knew that no amount of shouting or spear throwing would make the least bit of difference to him. As he approached the town, this is exactly what the guards of Megalise discovered.

Megalise's walls might have been big, but they were old, and no match for this troll. Just three blows from his huge fists sent them all tumbling the ground, while the terrified guards scattered in all directions. Delighted, the troll stepped over the rubble and made for the town square. Once he was there he shouted as loudly as he could.

'Where does Coop live?!'

In no time at all he was inundated with trembling townsfolk, eager to lead him to Coop and away from their own houses. It was not long before the troll was at Coop's door.

'Coop!' he bellowed. 'Come out Coop!'

Inside, Coop the coward had no intention of doing any such thing.

'You've taken my step daughter away from me, Coop, and I want my revenge!' the troll continued. 'Come out and fight me! I will spare your town if I can give you your just deserts!'

Inside, the confused Coop still had no intention of going to fight the troll at his door. He didn't want his just deserts. Outside, this became apparent as Coop continued to fail to appear.

'Very well,' the troll snarled, 'unless you come and fight me tomorrow I'll eat your whole town right up, and then I'll come for you. What do you have to say about that?'

Still Coop the coward said nothing. The troll stamped his foot and stomped off back to his cave. Coop listened as the colossal footsteps faded into the distance, and then, ignoring the frantic hammering of his neighbours on his door, he set about packing a bag as fast as he could.

He had nearly finished when he noticed that the hammering on his door had been replaced by a smaller, nervous knocking. He stopped and listened. There it was again. Against his better judgement he got up and opened the door.

There, on his doorstep, stood a doleful Belle.

'What is it?'

Coop had no idea what else to say.

'Please,' Belle said, 'can I come in? I have a lot to tell you.'

It was a long morning for Coop. He listened as his new love confessed to him that she was the step daughter of a troll, and he especially listened when she told him that she had fallen in love with him, and had now put him in grave danger.

She was the daughter of fairies, she said, who, thinking her to be a troll because of her unusual size and unable to care for her, had given her to the troll to raise when she was very young. The troll had done so on the condition that he could treat her as a slave, otherwise, he said, he would leave her to die. Not wishing any harm to come to their daughter, the fairies had agreed, but had made the troll promise that when she cam of age her debt would be cleared and he would let her go. But when she'd become old enough to leave the troll wouldn't let her, and eventually she had escaped, coming to Megalise in the hope of starting a better life. But her step father had followed her, and being a vengeful and spiteful troll, was sure to take her back, destroying the whole of Megalise, and especially Coop, in the process.

'Well,' said Coop, and then stopped, for he really couldn't think of anything else to say.

Belle looked at him expectantly, waiting for a brilliant plan, one that would see her free of her monstrous step father and, more importantly, free to live the rest of her life with the one good man she had ever met.

'Well,' Coop said again, and he licked his lips.

And then he picked up his bag and fled.

Belle watched him go, too angry to say a word.

Coop ran and ran and ran. He didn't know where he was going, but he did know that it was imperative that he put as much distance between himself and that troll before the next morning. Coop was no fighter, and he certainly wasn't brave. It was best to forget about Belle, there was no question about that. She had lied to him after all and gotten him into this mess in the first place.

But forgetting about someone you love more than anyone else in the whole world was harder than Coop had imagined. He really had to work at it. And as he ran he worked at it so hard that he never even noticed as he ran out of the Great Plains that surrounded Megalise and into the ice floes where the Necromancer and the Great Poisonous Snow Serpent lived. And he never had so much of an inkling of what was happening as a gnarly old fist came down and knocked what little senses he still had clean out of him.

Coop woke up in the Necromancer's cave with a splitting headache. His hands and feet were bound and from where he lay if he twisted his head hard enough he could see the Necromancer making a fire. He groaned. He knew all about the Necromancer. Everyone did. The Necromancer was more feared than trolls, and rightly so. He was the reason no one ever ventured into the ice floes, for to cross his path was certain death.

'Tell me,' the Necromancer said, turning round and approaching Coop, toying with what Coop noticed in alarm was easily the largest knife he had ever seen, 'what were you running from? It must have been something very scary indeed.'

'Well,' Coop admitted, 'that was an accident. I didn't meant to disturb you....'

And then he thought, well, if this is it, I might as well tell my story to someone, even if it is a murderous Necromancer. I might as well explain myself.

And so he did. Coop told the Necromancer all about Belle and how he loved her and of the consequences of her unfortunate step parentage. He told him how even though Belle had omitted certain key facts about her past he had no doubt that he had found true love with her and he longed for her even now but a crazed troll wanted to kill him and a crazed Necromancer *was* going to kill him.

But the Necromancer didn't kill him.

'If you love her as you say you do,' he asked, 'why did you run?'

Coop shook his head sadly.

'If I thought that there was any chance I could kill that troll I would have stayed. If there had been any point at all I wouldn't have run.'

He sighed. The Necromancer raised his knife.

True to his word, the troll reappeared at Coop's house the next day at exactly the same time.

'Coop!' he boomed. 'Coop!'

If there had been anyone left in the town, and if any of them had known about Coop's unfortunate meeting with The Necromancer, there would have been a lot more people around to be surprised at what happened next. As it was, it was only Belle who was there to give a gasp of shock as Coop's front door unclosed and Coop emerged.

The troll stepped back in surprise.

'So, you've come to face me like a man have you? Well, I must admit you're a lot braver than I had at first thought.'

'I'm not,' Coop answered, 'but I do love Belle.'

This answer annoyed the troll, but delighted Belle, who let out a gasp of excitement.

'What's that you're carrying?' the troll asked.

'It's a bow and arrow,' said Coop. 'Are we allowed weapons?'

The troll looked at the flimsy little thing the funny man was carrying. Anyone could see that it would never be enough to pierce his hide, which was as tough as dragon scales. Where was the harm?

'Very well,' the troll said. 'You can have one shot, and then I get to rip your head off. How does that sound?'

'That sounds fair,' said Coop. 'May I shoot now?'

'By all means,' the troll replied graciously.

Coop carefully fitted the arrow to the string of the bow, taking care not to cut himself with the sharp arrow head. He steadied his aim as much as he could through his trembling and took aim. Despite herself, Belle hid her head in her hands and let out another gasp.

'That's not helping,' Coop said.

Before Belle had time to reply he let the arrow fly. It sang through the air, and only ever so slightly changed course as it brushed the troll's arm on its way to bury itself in a neighbour's house beyond.

The troll couldn't help but laugh.

'You didn't even hit me!' he called incredulously as he strode towards Coop.

But he never made it to Coop. He hadn't taken more than two steps when a strange gurgling sound came from his throat. His eyes rolled back in his head and he surprised everyone, especially himself, by keeling over, quite dead.

When the dust had settled Belle stood up, far too surprised to gasp anymore.

Coop had to admit that he was a little taken aback himself. And once Belle had run to him and they had kissed and thoroughly made up he explained to her the Necromancer's plan.

Coop had been extraordinarily lucky when the Necromancer had caught him for three reasons. The first was that the Necromancer had just that morning killed a poor unsuspecting traveller and had added another skull to his collection, so wasn't really feeling any urgent need for another one. The second was that he was on his way to kill the Great Poisonous Snow Serpent, hence the big knife. And the third was that, if there was anything the Necromancer valued more in the world than the skulls of his victims, it was true love.

Coop's story had touched the Necromancer's black heart, and he had resolved to help the troll crossed lovers. He had set off without further ado and slain the Great Poisonous Snow Serpent and returned with a vial of its blood, more poisonous than anything else on this earth. He had then taken a bow and arrow and dipped the tip of the arrow in the blood. He told Coop to shoot the arrow at the troll, and provided that he didn't miss completely, the poison would kill him. It was true that no arrow could pierce a troll's hide, but it was equally true that it didn't need to if it had been dipped in the blood of the Great Poisonous Snow Serpent. The poison would do its work, even through thick troll skin.

And so it had. With Belle's step father dead, Coop and Belle were now free to live as they pleased, and stayed happily together in Megalise in for the rest of their days. And from that day forth Coop was no longer a coward. He had learnt to stand up for himself and for others, and from that day forth that is exactly what he did. When the residents of Megalise returned to their town he no longer tolerated their dishonesty and thievery, and forced them to change their ways. And they listened to him. And so Megalise became a place that people wanted to live, and it prospered, and as far as anyone knows, it still prospers to this day.

Prince Head

Darryl arrived in Bert one summer's morning. He had come to visit a friend whom he hadn't seen in quite some time. He'd never been to Bert before, and walked slowly to the main square, looking about him curiously at the place as he did so.

'I wonder,' Darryl ventured aloud to no one in particular, 'I wonder how old some of these houses might be. This town looks truly ancient.'

And ancient it was. Crooked spires beckoned from tumbledown roofs, cats played in half buried ruins, and children skipped over cobblestones that had borne the feet of scores of generations before them. Visitors didn't often come to Bert, and Darryl got more than one strange look from the townsfolk as he sauntered by.

It was a warm day, with the type of sun that made everything sing. Darryl was in no rush at all – his was a journey of leisure, and he ambled slowly towards the main square, drinking in the sights of this new town. It was dominated by a huge ruined castle that stood on a hill above the houses, and as Darryl gazed up at the hulking stone walls he found himself hypnotised. It was many hundreds of years old by the look of it, now slowly crumbling into nothing, and for a fan of old ruins as Darryl was it couldn't have been more perfect.

He basked in the sunshine in the town square for a full hour before deciding to find his friend's house. He rose slowly, savouring the warmth in his limbs from the sunlight, and made his way through the streets in what he thought was the right direction. He soon found himself thoroughly lost, for the streets twisted this way and that like a great mass of cobbled serpents, and Darryl found himself turning first one way and then another in an effort to keep his bearings. It didn't much matter to him which direction he took, he never seemed to end up where he thought he would. He started to get frustrated, and then agitated, for he began to feel very uncomfortable whenever he found himself walking with his back to the castle.

After nearly an hour of becoming thoroughly lost he turned a particularly sharp corner to see a small, pale man cowering in a nearby alley shadow. In his surprise he pulled up sharp, and it wasn't until the man spoke that he realised who he was.

'I thought it was you,' the man said. 'I've been watching you from my bedroom window for some time.'

'Paul!'

Darryl clapped the man on the back, making him wince.

'Well here you are, what luck! I have to confess, I was beginning to wonder if I was ever going to find you.'

'Oh no,' Paul replied, 'We'll be safe enough here as anywhere else.'

And with this slightly odd response he turned and opened the front door to a nearby house, conducting Darryl with the manner of one ushering in a fugitive, peering about him all the time.

'Of course,' he continued once they were safely inside, 'you don't mean to stay here do you?'

'I certainly do!' Darryl replied. 'Just as I said in my letter. It's been too long, old friend. This is a charming town, and I can stay here for a few days at least if you'll have me. I'm in no rush at all. That is,' he added hesitantly, seeing the look on his friend's face, 'if you have room for me.'

At this Paul seemed to remember himself and smiled back at his friend.

'Of course I have room for you. Forgive me, I haven't been myself these last few days, and have had some nasty frights if you want to know the truth. But let me show you to your room, you're welcome to stay for as long as you like.'

On the way up to his room Darryl pondered the change that had come over his friend. The Paul he knew was cheerful and carefree, not this timid, nervous man who seemed scared of his own shadow. What had happened? Their journey up the stairs together was peppered by furtive glances left and right from Paul, who jumped at every creak and trembled at every dark corner. And in his own home, no less!

At the very top of the house they finally reached Darryl's room. It was certainly a generous size, and Darryl saw with great joy that it afforded him a magnificent view of the castle.

'What do you know about that place?' he asked Paul as he gazed out at the ruin.

'The castle?' Paul asked, casting a fearful look in its direction. 'Why, it's stood empty for hundreds of years. It used to be owned by Prince Head, master of these parts a long time ago, but the castle hasn't been occupied since then.'

This interested Darryl.

'Why not?' he asked.

'It's hard to say. The prince was by all accounts obsessed with youth, and practised a type of black magic if you believe in that kind of thing. He was said to have said that he would gladly make a pact with the devil himself if he could be young forever. And, so the story goes, he was in his room one night doing something he no doubt shouldn't have with spells and potions and the like when his servants heard a terrible scream. They ran to see what was the matter, but when they got to his room the Prince had disappeared. He was never heard from or seen again since – he seemed to have just vanished into thin air. No one wanted to live in the castle much after that. There was talk of shadows and a kind of darkness about the place. It's said that strange things started happening there, laughter coming from empty rooms, footsteps in empty corridors and the like. It's been deserted ever since.'

'I'd very much like to visit it,' said Darryl. 'Come on, it's still early, would you be able to take me there?'

At this Paul hesitated.

'Well, yes I would, I've been there many times myself. I was there just a few days ago in fact. But I really wouldn't recommend it, I hardly think – '

'Come on!'

Paul was hesitant, but Darryl wouldn't take no for an answer, and quickly wore down his friend's half hearted protests. They were just turning to leave the room when something caught Paul's eye, and he stopped dead where he was, staring at something lying in the corner of the room.

His gaze had been caught by a small silver pendant, about the same size and shape as a coin, with a rough bit old of string running through a hole in the top of it. Intrigued, Darryl went and picked it up, while Paul stayed where he was, breathing very fast.

Ignoring his friend, Darryl took the pendant over to the window to have a closer look. It was charming, he thought, and very old. The silver disc was covered with the most exquisite patterns, the like of which Darryl had never seen before. It was stunning, but it was when Darryl turned it over to have a look at the other side that his breath was really taken away.

The other face to the pendant was quite different. This had no patterns on at all, but instead bore the image of a figure that made Darryl's skin crawl. It was a man, or at least something like a man, and was standing in a kind of half crouch, as if waiting to pounce. The figure was wearing what looked like robes and was hooded, with only half of its face visible, which was more than enough for Darryl. Even in miniature it was a face that filled Darryl was a feeling of dread. The jaw was twisted into a cruel, mocking grin, and the nose was hooked and cruel. But it was the one eye that was visible from the shadow of the hood that was the thing that took Darryl's breath away. It seemed to stare right out of the pendant, right into him, and he found himself staring back, transfixed. In the corner Paul gave a low moan.

And then suddenly Darryl's reverie broke. Sunlight seemed to flood the room with renewed vigour, and the pendant in his hand was just a trinket once more. He waved it in front of Paul's face.

'What's this then? Funny little thing, isn't it?'

Paul looked sick.

'I – it's from the castle, I took it from there a few days ago. I thought I'd thrown it away, but….'

He trailed off, looking for all the world like he was going to faint.

Darryl looked at it again.

'I'll take it off your hands if you don't want it.'

'No!'

Paul's answer was immediate, and he snatched it from Darryl's hand with a speed that shocked Darryl.

'I wasn't going to steal it!'

At this Paul looked even more terrified.

'You don't want to take it from me, old friend, believe me, you don't.'

And that seemed to be the end of the matter.

The two men spoke little on the way to the castle. Darryl, still entranced by Bert, was happily lost in the sights and sounds of the old town as they passed through it, and Paul seemed to be by turns brooding, terrified, and distracted. When they reached the ruin Darryl was delighted to find that it was all he had hoped and much more. The stone of the walls wasn't in as nearly a bad condition as it looked from the town, and they were all covered in the strangest carvings, almost like runes. Darryl was fascinated, and was sorry they hadn't come up here earlier.

It was a hot, sunny day, yet the castle felt somehow cool; Darryl reasoned that it was probably the exposed aspect of the place that accounted for the temperature, despite there not being any wind. They spent hours exploring every nook and canny of the ruin, clambering over fallen columns and inspecting every decoration and carving. All this time Paul kept close at Darryl's heels, as if scared to let him out of his sight. The poor man was a bag of nerves, and as pale as a ghost.

Eventually they came to rest at the doorway of an abandoned tower. Darryl was just inwardly debating their next move, and marvelling at the trembling of Paul, when he heard what sounded like thin, tinny laughter coming from the top of it. They knew that there could be no question of anyone being up there, for they had in fact just come down themselves, and Darryl shot a quizzical look at Paul, who jumped almost fair out of his skin.

'That's no one – I mean nothing,' he said, looking sick. 'I think we should go now, I can make you a supper back at the house if you'd like.'

Darryl had to confess that he was hungry, and so they made the short descent back to the town.

For all his nerves, Paul was an excellent host, and the two ate a delicious meal and talked well into the night. The conversation seemed to do Paul a great deal of good, so much so that when Darryl repeated his wish to stay for a few days he didn't hesitate at all, but told him that he must. Regrettably he had some business that needed attending to in town over the next few days, but he was sure that Darryl would be able to occupy himself. Darryl agreed, and after one final nightcap the two retired for the night, both feeling that special kind of contentment that only comes from catching up with old friends.

Before Darryl went to bed he stood at his bedroom window for some time, gazing at the dark hulk of the castle on its hill. He was interrupted from his reverie by what sounded like a short, sharp gasp coming from the direction of Paul's room. Curious, he went to his door and put his ear to it, listening for any further noises from his host's room, but he heard nothing more. Quickly getting bored of his attempted eavesdropping he took himself to bed and fell into a dreamless sleep.

The next day Paul was out working, and Darryl decided to spend the day wandering around on his own, admiring this pretty little town. He couldn't have been happier, and resolved to do the same the next day as well. He arrived home ravenous, and, as he had done the night before, Paul cooked a wonderful supper for his guest.

The food, wine and conversation were all excellent, and as the two friends ate Darryl was starting to think that maybe he'd like to stay for even longer when he looked across the table and saw that same look of terror on Paul's face that he'd seen on the day he arrived. He followed Paul's frightened stare and saw that he was looking once more at that same pendant, which was now hanging from a picture hook on the wall behind him.

'How?' Paul stammered to himself.

'Look, if that thing worries you so much, I'll take it off your hands,' Darryl told his friend, wondering why he'd hung it on the wall when he evidently didn't like it.

'No! No no no.'

Paul ran over and took the pendant from the wall and slipped it into his pocket once more.

'I assure you, it wouldn't interest you.'

'I like it,' Darryl told him. 'There wouldn't be one for sale like it anywhere it town would there?'

'I'm afraid there wouldn't be,' replied Paul, who was by now as white as a sheet, and he turned and scuttled out of the room as if all hell were at his heels, muttering something about washing the dishes.

That night Darryl found it hard to sleep, for his mind kept coming back to the pendant, and Paul's curious reaction to it. As he lay in the dark puzzling it over he thought that he heard, very faintly, the same thin laughter that he had heard in the castle. He held his breath again, listening to the dark, but the sound didn't come again. He fancied that it had come from the direction of Paul's room. Slowly he rose, and made his way to the door. He poked his head out into the hallway but there was no one there, and Paul's door remained firmly shut, with the just flickering light of a candle visible underneath. As Darryl looked at the thin bar of light at the base of the door he saw something pass across it, something black, like the hem of a gown. A sudden fear took hold of him and he ducked back into his room, hoping that he hadn't been seen. He spent the rest of the night in a state of some anxiety, and it was the early hours of the morning before he finally got to sleep.

He woke early, however, and the first thing that popped into his head was the pendant. As he was leaving the house he met Paul, and he asked this time if he could buy it from him. This seemed to throw Paul into a larger than usual state of agitation, and the answer was a most definite no.

Darryl passed a thoroughly boring day, having exhausted the possibilities of Bert, and he came back early in a foul mood. He'd found his thoughts consumed by the pendant, and he began to resent Paul for not selling or giving it to him. It really was most unfair, he thought. He barely said a word to his friend over dinner, which only served to compound Paul's misery. After the meal Darryl stayed up brooding, sitting on his own in an armchair while Paul tidied up and attempted to make small talk.

'Are you alright?' Paul asked timidly.

'I'm not feeling well,' Darryl replied irritably. 'I think it might be best if I leave tomorrow.'

Paul looked concerned.

'I'll call the doctor first thing tomorrow. It may have been that trip to the castle, I don't think that place is healthy.'

'There's no need for that,' Darryl snapped. 'I'll be perfectly fine, I just need a change of scenery, that's all.'

His friend made no attempt to reply to this, and left Darryl glowering in the corner. Paul was evidently preparing to go upstairs to go to bed, and as Darryl watched he took the little pendant out of his pocket and put it in a drawer before going upstairs to his room.

What luck! Darryl couldn't believe it. He waited with bated breath until Paul went upstairs, and then ran to the drawer and stole the pendant, putting it on and tucking it inside his shirt. No sooner had he done so then he heard his friend coming downstairs again, and in alarm he leapt back into his chair as if nothing had happened. Paul entered, picked up his hat that he had left behind and then went back upstairs, whistling. In fact, although he had only been in the room for a total of a few seconds Darryl got the impression of a man from whom a great weight had been lifted. He walked straighter, even with a spring in his step, and not once did he cast about him nervously as Darryl had grown accustomed to seeing him do over the last few days.

But Darryl didn't give this any thought. As soon as he heard his friend's door close he retired to his own room, crowing with delight at his cleverness.

Once there he turned all the lamps on, for he was suddenly very afraid of the dark. A sense of being watched had seemed to come over him, and he found himself looking over his shoulder a number of times as he had seen Paul do habitually. Finally, after roaming around the room for some time, checking under the bed and closing the window, he settled down in a chair to examine his prize. As he drew the pendant out from his shirt he was surprised to find that all the time against his skin hadn't warmed the metal at all; it was still quite cool.

It made sense that Paul had found it in the castle, for the abstract decorations on it were of the same type that he had seen carved everywhere on the walls up there. It was clearly ancient, and Darryl wouldn't have been surprised if it was even older than the castle. He turned it over to have a look at the other face again, the one with the figure on it. It really was a horrible thing, Darryl thought, this crouched hooded figure. Why had he wanted it so much? The picture was grotesque. Perplexed as to why it had ever entered his head to take such a thing, Darryl let the pendant fall once more against his chest, suddenly bored with it. He then looked at the wall in front of him and saw a shadow where before there had been none.

The sight was so utterly unexpected that Darryl couldn't at first work out what he was looking at. The shadow cast on the wall wasn't of anything that was in his room, yet the shape of it was something that he had seen before. He realised, with a slow horror, that the shadow of the thing standing behind him was the same shape as that terrible figure on the pendant. And worse still, the figure seemed to be moving, rising from its dreadful crouch. With a cry, Darryl leapt up and turned to face whatever it might be.

Paul left Bert a few days later, back to his old cheerful self, seemingly without a care in the world. Darryl, on the other hand, found that he was too ill to go anywhere. He had suffered a great shock, but what this shock was no one, least of all Darryl himself, could say. Paul was insistent to anyone who would listen that there was nothing he could do to help his friend, and that the best thing he could do for him was to leave him alone. He seemed to be in a great hurry to get away from the place, and left as soon as he could.

Darryl continued to live in Paul's old house until his untimely death, which I am sorry to say came not long after Paul's departure. His new neighbours found that Darryl was a sickly, timid man, who was frightened of his own shadow. He would never say how he came by it, but he was constantly trying to give away a curious old pendant that he carried about with him, although no one ever wanted a piece of old tat like that. A few of them, knowing that he wasn't well, would pop in to see him from time to time, and they often find him staring at it, muttering to himself and staring at it in disbelief. He used to tell them in his more lucid moments that it would be the death of him, muttering that if he hadn't stolen it the prince would have let him be, but no one ever thought to ask what he meant by that.

The Dolls' House

Beyond the woods, beyond the seas, beyond high mountains, there is a town called Ridge that was once a happy and vibrant place. It was home to a good number of people, young and old, and all were as friendly and kind to one another as could be. The richer citizens looked after the poorer ones, and the young would look after the old, who in turn would share their wisdom generously. Fighting and jealousy were unheard of, and the town grew from strength to strength.

Right in the centre of Ridge, in a big house with a red front door, lived a man called Mr Stephen. In a town of popular people, he was the most popular by far, for he was a sorcerer, and loved nothing more than to amaze and excite his fellow townsfolk with tricks of magic. He was a tremendous show off, and his greatest pleasure was to be the centre of attention.

Mr Stephen was also a woodturner of great skill, and carving furniture and toys for children was how he made his living. His skill was well known far and wide.

One night, as Mr Stephen sat alone in his workshop finishing off a particularly lifelike doll, an idea came to him. The doll was about the height of a child, with fully working arms and legs, and even jointed fingers and toes. So realistically had Mr Stephen painted it that a passer by could well be forgiven for thinking that a real child was sitting on his workbench. This thought occurred to Mr Stephen, and he thought how delightful it would be if the doll really would come to life. How people would be amazed! Carried away with such imaginings, Mr Stephen set aside his hammer and chisel and breathed life into his creation.

At first nothing happened. But then Mr Stephen saw one of the doll's legs twitch, and then the other. Then its arms started to move. Finally, it turned its head around to face Mr Stephen, and it smiled.

Mr Stephen was beside himself. What a thing, a living doll! He quickly picked up the newly living toy that was still blinking uncertainly at the world around it, and locked it in a cupboard and went up to bed rubbing his hands with glee. The next day he got up early and built a large pen outside his house.

'Whatever are you doing?' asked his curious neighbours, as he darted around like a madman with hammer and nails, making something that looked for all the world like a sheep pen to them. 'You don't own any sheep.'

'Just you wait and see,' grinned Mr Stephen. 'Just you wait!'

When he'd finished he ran inside and unlocked the cupboard. He grabbed the doll and put it in the middle of the pen, where it sat looking this way and that, unsure of what to do.

'Roll up, roll up!' cried Mr Stephen. 'Come and see the amazing living doll! Wonder at what I have done!'

He didn't have to ask twice. Soon a crowd of people were thronging around the pen, pointing and exclaiming at the doll that had by now got to its feet and was walking around its enclosure. Children squealed, women cooed, and men rushed to shake Mr Stephen by the hand. What a wonderful thing! What a marvel! Could be make another?

But of course! Mr Stephen ran inside and immediately set to work making more dolls. By tea time, six more had joined his first effort in the pen, all walking around trying to make sense of what was going on. The crowd's appetite for these living toys was insatiable, and Mr Stephen added more dolls to the pen daily. He then hit upon an idea – children could play with them! He built a small gate in the pen and let the children of the town in to play with the dolls. It was a great success. The children loved their wooden playmates, and the dolls soon learned from their human visitors how to play and act just like real children. They'd been getting bored in their pen, and having children to play with seemed to cheer them up no end.

Mr Stephen's dolls were the talk of the town all that summer, and every day the queue of children to play with the dolls was bigger than the day before. Everyone agreed it was the most marvellous thing, and Mr Stephen couldn't go anywhere without someone stopping him to tell him how clever he was, which suited him just fine.

It was a few weeks before the first child was hurt. As usual, the pen was full of children and dolls, all playing tig and catch and skipping together, when suddenly one of the dolls went to tag a little girl and hit her hard on the head with his wooden hand. He thought nothing of it, and ran off before he could be tagged back, but the little girl fell to the ground crying and holding her head. Her anxious mother immediately ran into the pen and carried her out, and Mr Stephen of course was mortified. But nothing like this had happened before, and he was confident that it wouldn't happen again.

Sadly, he was to be proved very wrong. A few days later a doll threw a ball hard at a young boy, nearly breaking his arm, and a few days after that another little girl was whipped with a skipping rope by a doll. Frightened parents stopped taking their children to play with the dolls.

'It's not their fault,' Mr Stephen's pleaded, 'they don't understand that not everyone's made out of wood like them. They'll learn.'

But the parents weren't taking any chances, and soon the dolls found themselves alone again in their pen. Mr Stephen noticed that they no longer wandered around aimlessly as they had done when he had first put them in the enclosure, but they now sat together, as if conferring. Once or twice he caught one of them trying to climb out of the pen, and as a precaution he made it an extra foot higher.

Mr Stephen wasn't a cruel man, and he saw that perhaps the dolls were getting bored. He threw balls and skipping ropes and spinning tops into the pen, and even built a slide for them to play on, but nothing seemed to hold their attention for very long. He sometimes tried to go in and play with them himself, but every time he opened the pen's gate a doll would try to run out.

'You want to be free, don't you?' he said one day to his first doll, whom he had nicknamed Mike. 'But where would you go?'

Mike didn't answer, but just looked back at him with his living wooden eyes.

A few nights later Mr Stephen was woken by a terrible scream coming from next door. Hurriedly throwing on some clothes, he rushed downstairs and ran to his neighbours. He didn't notice in the darkness that the doll's pen was empty.

When he got to the house next door he was greeted by a dreadful scene. The children were sitting outside on the street, crying and nursing a great many fresh bruises, and there were sounds of a struggle going on inside the house. Before Mr Stephen's horrified eyes the front door opened and a doll emerged, dragging the children's mother out of the house by her hair while she screamed fit to burst. The father was next, carried out of his own house by two dolls. The dolls flung father and mother into the street, and then went back inside and shut the door.

Appalled, Mr Stephen ran to the front door and hammered on it for all he was worth. It was opened by one of his dolls, who stood looking at him, its painted smile looking redder than ever in the flickering lamplight from inside.

'What are you doing?' Mr Stephen cried. 'This isn't right! This isn't how we treat each other!'

The doll simply stared back at him and shut the door again.

Mr Stephen became aware that he could hear more screams and fighting going on all around him. Right across town the story was the same – the dolls were breaking into people's houses and throwing them out. By dawn they had occupied every house, and the battered residents gathered in the town square, dismissed from their own homes.

'This is an outrage!' said one particularly hot headed young man. 'Are we going to stand for this? Are we really going to let children's playthings keep us from our own houses? Not if I have anything to do with it!'

The crowd cheered, and the menfolk of the town sallied back to their houses with torches and pitchforks to take back what was theirs.

'Please don't hurt them!' cried Mr Stephen. 'They just want to be free!'

But no one listened to him.

When the men attacked the houses the dolls were ready for them. They dropped boiling oil onto them from upstairs windows, and threw pots and pans and anything else they could find from the rooftops. The men couldn't get anywhere near their homes, and not one house was reclaimed.

And so the residents of Ridge were left no choice but to leave their beloved town and wander in search of a new site to call home. They roamed for many years, and eventually they settled not far from here. The town of Ridge still stands, but no one visits it any more, save for a luckless traveller every now and then who will stumble upon it, not knowing what the place is. Such unwitting travellers find themselves in a pen outside a large house with a red front door, while dolls queue for a turn to play with them.

The Magic Whistle

There was once an old childless couple who lived in a tiny house on the edge of a small village in a kingdom far, far away. They had just one neighbour, a witch, who lived by herself in a tall, dark house. The couple, like everyone else, had never met her, but everyone knew how evil she was. All who lived nearby were terrified of her, and people would walk miles out of their way just so that they wouldn't have to walk past her house. The mere thought of her was enough to send shivers down anyone's spine, but she had never bothered her neighbours, and they lived quietly enough in her shadow.

The couple longed for a child more than anything else in the world, but their prayers were never answered, and they had to content themselves with an old cat and a dog that had lived with them for many years. Theirs was a comfortable existence. They made money by selling bread to the rest of the village and farming in the nearby fields, and made a very good living from it, but the absence of a son or daughter meant that they never felt truly happy.

One day the husband was walking home from a day tending to his crops when, at a crossroads that he had passed a thousand times before, he saw a curious thing lying on the ground. He picked it up and looked at it. It was a rusty old whistle, quite plain and boring looking. The man blew on it, and suddenly a small sprite appeared before him, hopping from foot to foot with mischievous glee. The man was so startled that he jumped back, dropping the whistle in his fright.

'Well, hello!' laughed the sprite. 'And what can I do for you?'

'What can you do for me?' the man asked in confusion.

'You tell me,' the sprite countered with a glint in his eye. 'You blew on my whistle and summoned me here. I can and will give you whatever your heart most desires. I can grant one wish, and one wish only, so think hard about what you might ask.'

'Anything at all?' the old man could scarce believe his luck.

'Oh, yes,' the sprite told him. 'I will grant you whatever you desire, but in return you must give me a piece of you to eat.'

'What?!' the smile instantly left the man's face. 'I will do no such thing. You won't eat a single part of me. Go away you horrible little beast.'

'Oh, I'm sorry to hear that,' said the sprite, hopping up onto the man's shoulder to speak closely into his ear. 'If I must go hungry, then I won't leave you. You summoned me after all, and I'll go nowhere until I'm promised a portion of your tasty flesh to eat.'

And so saying the sprite bit down hard upon the man's ear, causing him to howl with pain while the sprite sat on his shoulder and laughed his tinkling little laugh.

Frightened, the man started off home once more, holding his ear and hurrying as fast as he could in an effort to lose the sprite. But no matter how fast he went the sprite wouldn't leave him. Not only that, but the sprite was intent on causing him all manner of misery, pulling his beard, twisting his nose, pinching the backs of his knees and kicking and punching him whenever he could. The poor man was beside himself by the time he got home, but the sprite wouldn't leave him alone even then, flying in through the door with him before he had time to do anything about it.

'Whatever is that?' asked his bewildered wife, as the sprite jumped up onto a shelf in the kitchen and started dropping plates one by one where they smashed onto the stone floor.

'He - he followed me home,' stammered her distressed husband. 'I couldn't get rid of him!'

'He summoned me,' corrected the sprite as he threw around pots and pans, narrowly missing the old man's head.

And so the miserable man told his wife all about the whistle he had found and the sprite's impossible demand, while the sprite hopped about from room to room, laughing and breaking everything and making such a mess as you have never seen in all your life. He only stopped to pop his head back into the kitchen and grin wickedly at the terrified couple.

'You don't have any children, do you?' he asked. 'I do enjoy children, they're ever so tasty.'

For the first time in their lives the couple were glad that they were childless.

Days turned into weeks and weeks turned into months, but still the sprite wouldn't leave the poor couple alone. They were terrorized day and night, and they were soon covered in bruises and scars from his biting and pinching and blows. Sometimes the sprite would follow the man out to the fields where he went to work, sometimes he would stay at home with the wife, torturing her and breaking everything he could in the house.

The couple were black and blue and bleary eyed, but somehow, in the midst of all of this, the wife found that she was pregnant. They had been dreaming of this for many years, but now a chill of terror went through them both, for they knew that as soon as the child was born the sprite would eat it. They tried to hide the fact from him, but as time went on the sprite noticed of course, and he licked his lips with delight.

'A child!' he exclaimed. 'I shall eat that up as soon as it appears. What a tasty little snack for me!'

The couple were beside themselves, and didn't know what to do. Finally, the man, tortured by the thought of what might happen to the child that he and his wife had waited so long for, did an unthinkable thing – he went to see the witch next door.

Her house was a darksome place, and the man trembled as he climbed the steps to her porch. The very air felt thick and stale. As he raised his hand to knock, the door suddenly opened, and before

64

him stood the hunched shape of the witch. She looked right into him with steely eyes.

'I – I beg pardon,' the man stammered, too frightened to even talk properly, 'you see, I, I mean we –'

'I know why you're here!' the witch snapped.

'Do you?' the man hadn't expected this.

'Of course I do!' the reply was barked and hard. 'Now come in, quickly, before your horrible little friend sees where you are.'

And so the man was ushered into the witch's house. It was an old, dank place, full of cobwebs and darkness. There was little light, despite the fact that it was a fine day outside. Toads croaked in corners, and cracked, dusty mirrors hung on equally cracked walls.

'How long have we been neighbours?' the witch wheeled around and looked at the man.

The man had to confess that he didn't know.

'Thirty years! And during that time, have you or your wife ever spoken to me, or taken any sort of an interest in me? Have you ever brought round cakes and rolls as I've seen you doing for your other friends, or offered to help me chop firewood when the weather became cold? No! And now you need my help. Well, I will help you, foolish man, but it won't be for free. I will tell you how to keep your child safe and get rid of that vicious little thing once and for all, but in return you must promise me that when your child is six years old you will give it to me, to raise as my own. Promise me this, and I shall do as I say.'

In haste the man agreed, so desperate was he to be rid of the sprite. And so, in hushed tones, the witch told him what to do, and he hurried home to tell his wife, forgetting all about the dreadful promise he had made.

After another month had gone by it was time for the wife to give birth. Following the witch's instructions the man managed to distract the sprite while his wife snuck out of the house and gave birth in secret, in a barn not far away. She then set her child down tenderly in a manger and picked up the biggest stone she could find. She wrapped it in swaddling clothes and hurried back to the house before the sprite had noticed that she'd gone. Once she got back she jumped into bed and her husband ran to join her in the bedroom and slammed the door. The sprite was downstairs, breaking things in the kitchen, but when he heard the door slam he ran up to see what was going on. When he got to the bedroom he found it locked.

'Let me in!' he shouted in a rage. 'Let me in or I'll beat you both black and blue!'

'My wife is giving birth!' the man shouted back from behind the door. 'Please, leave us be for just five minutes.'

The sprite was overjoyed, and stopped beating on the door immediately. After a little while the man opened the door and the sprite flew into the room. He picked up the huge stone wrapped in swaddling clothes and swallowed it whole, crowing as he did so.

'Tasty child!' he exclaimed, licking his lips, 'I do hope there are more where that came from.'

After such a big meal the sprite soon fell into a deep sleep. Then, as the witch had told them to do, the couple gently picked the sprite up, taking great care not to wake him, and carried him down to the river. Once there, they threw him in as hard as they could. The stone in the sprite's belly was so heavy that he sank to the bottom of the river and struggle as he might he stayed there, unable to make his way back up to the surface.

In peace at last, the couple were overjoyed, and quickly ran to the barn to recover their child. It was a baby girl, and she had suffered no harm at all from being left on her own. The witch had woven an enchantment around her, keeping her quite safe. They named her Vera and took her home, and a happier home you never did see.

But six years can pass very quickly, and when the witch knocked at the couple's door to claim what was rightfully hers she took both parents by surprise.

'It hasn't been six years!' the man cried in vain as the witch took the child from the mother's arms.

'Oh but it has,' replied the witch, 'and this child has been promised to me. Dare you go back on your word to me?'

'What is she talking about?' the confused mother asked her husband.

The man was forced to tell her of the promise he had made to save their daughter's life, and they both wept as the witch carried the child away. There was nothing that could be done, for neither of them dared to go back on a promise made to a witch.

The witch shut the young girl up in her house and built a great wall around it, so that no one could see in or out. She treated Vera most dreadfully; feeding her little and making her do all of the household chores day and night. The girl lived a pitiable existence, but as the years passed she nevertheless grew into a beautiful young woman.

In time the witch came to rely on her young slave more and more, and she would let Vera out into the nearby forest to collect firewood and run other errands for her. The girl never ran away, for the witch had promised her that she would take a terrible vengeance on her parents if she did, and in this way she kept total control over poor Vera. One such day, as she collected firewood for her captor, a young prince who was strolling through the forest saw her and fell instantly in love with her. Too shy to approach Vera, he followed her as she went home, and saw her enter the dark and forbidding home of the witch.

From that day forth the prince tarried outside the witch's house in the hope of seeing the beautiful girl again, but he never did. The witch had noticed this young man outside her walls and guessed what was going on. She never sent Vera out for firewood again, and the prince remained disappointed.

For many weeks the prince haunted the witch's house, and when he saw no sign of his beloved he decided to ask about her at the house next door. He was greeted by the old couple, now very old indeed, who explained all to him, and told him with tears in their eyes that sadly they were unable to help.

'But,' said the old man, there is perhaps one thing that you could try.'

'Why, I will try anything,' said the young prince, 'for your daughter is beautiful beyond compare, and I would do anything to see her again.'

'Very well,' said the old man with a heavy sigh. 'Directly north from here, not more than two miles away from the village, there is a crossroads. At that crossroads, if you look carefully on the floor, you may find the same old whistle I blew on many years ago that summoned the magical sprite and caused all of this trouble in the first place. Perhaps if you could call him he could grant this wish for you. However,' he continued, grasping the prince's shoulder, 'as I have told you, there is a dear price to pay, and I would urge you to think carefully before blowing upon the whistle.'

'I would gladly pay any price!' cried the prince, and immediately ran to find the instrument.

He had not travelled two miles from the village before the prince found the crossroads, just as the old man had said. He immediately fell upon the floor, searching for the whistle. He eventually found it, under a pile of leaves and feverishly put it to his lips and blew.

The note of the whistle had no sooner died down then the grinning little sprite appeared at his side, soaking wet and jumping up and down with glee.

'Free at last!' he cried.

The prince looked at this funny little creature.

'You called?' it asked, laughing a high pitched, tinkling little laugh.

'That depends,' replied the prince, 'can you help me?'

'It most certainly does not depend,' the sprite hopped from foot to foot, still laughing. 'You called me; there are no two ways about it. Yes, I can help you, but I must ask of you something in return. I can grant anything you wish, but you must give me a piece of you to eat in exchange for my favour.'

The prince thought about this.

'Do I get to choose which part?' he asked.

'Why, certainly you do,' replied the sprite.

'And do I get to choose when you may eat this part of me?' the prince asked.

'I don't see why not,' said the sprite.

'Then we have a deal,' the prince announced. 'I give you my word that before I die I will offer you the most precious piece of me to eat. In return, I would like you to free the young woman who is kept as a slave by the witch who lives next to the old couple at the edge of the village and bring her to me. Do this, and I swear I will uphold my end of the bargain.'

At this the sprite disappeared, leaving the prince alone in the darkening forest. With the sun setting, he made the long, lonely walk back to the old couple's house, where he told them all that had passed. He stayed with them that night, and the next night as well, but the sprite did not reappear. On the morning of the third day they were woken by a knock at the door. To their amazement, there stood Vera, with the sprite hopping up and down on her shoulder.

The old couple were beside themselves with joy, and with tears in their eyes they welcomed their daughter back home, embracing her as if they would never let go. To the prince's dismay, Vera didn't pay him a second glance, even when her parents thanked him from the bottom of their hearts. The sprite, of course, didn't leave, for he hadn't forgotten that he was still owed the prince's flesh.

And so they all stayed under the old couple's roof that night, and the next day the witch came knocking at the door, furious that her captive had been taken. The couple were quaking with fear, but the prince hid their daughter in a cupboard, and thus saved them all from the witch's fury.

'I cannot see her,' said the witch, 'but I know that that girl is here somewhere. I won't stop looking, and when I find her here I will make you all wish you had never been born!'

True to her word, the witch came back the next day. This time, the prince hid Vera in a basket, and again the witch did not find her. She came again the next day, and this time Vera hid herself under a bed, and still the witch did not find her.

It was obvious that the witch would never stop hunting, and so the prince approached the sprite once more.

'Sprite,' he said, 'I will give you another piece of me to eat right now if you will kill that witch and rid us of her once and for all.'

And so saying he held out his little finger to the sprite who bit it off greedily.

'Certainly I will do that,' he said as he licked his lips, and he disappeared in a trice.

The witch never bothered them again, and the four of them lived very happily under the one roof together for many months. The prince had a home elsewhere, but his love and devotion for Vera wouldn't let him leave her. He tried everything he could to win her affection, but sadly she found that she couldn't love him back. Finally, the four fingered prince had to return to his father's kingdom, and he asked Vera for her hand in marriage. She looked at him with sorrow.

'Noble prince,' she said, 'I'm sorry, but try as I might I don't love you as you love me. My parents, I know, love you as they would a son. I myself owe you everything. Yet it would be far better for you to go back to your castle and marry a noblewoman there who will love you, for I cannot.'

The heartbroken prince left the old couple's house and returned to his castle, where, after some years, he became king. He never did marry. The old couple and their daughter for their part lived most happily in their little cottage on the edge of the village, finally able to enjoy the life they had always dreamed of.

Many years past, and the young king became an old man. As he lay on his deathbed the sprite appeared before him once more, hopping from foot to foot as usual, and laughing that twinkly little laugh of his.

'I do hope,' said the sprite, 'that you haven't forgotten your promise to me. I believe that I am still owed a part of you to eat.'

The old king smiled.

'Oh yes,' he said, 'once I have breathed my final breath you may have my heart, the most precious piece of me I can offer.'

The sprite threw back his head and laughed for joy.

'You are too kind!' he said to the king. 'Really, you are.'

But the king didn't reply, for life had finally left him.

With a crow of triumph the sprite jumped onto the king's body and opened his chest. But his laughter soon turned to howls of rage and frustration, for the king's heart was nowhere to be found. The sprite hopped up and down and gnashed his teeth but it was no good - the heart wasn't there.

Sprites are not like us, they are cruel and greedy creatures who feel no love for anyone, and so the angry little man jumping up and down couldn't possibly have understood that the king had known all along that his heart wouldn't be there. It was with Vera, as it had been from the moment he had first seen her collecting wood in the forest all those years ago. And even though she couldn't return his love, he would not have had it back for all the world.

The Trouble with Fairies

Bost was a young boy of eight years old who lived with his mother in a small house by the sea. He loved his mother very much, and never once gave her any cause for complaint. Bost never lied, cheated or stole, he always ate all the food on his plate and he always did as he was told.

Not that Bost's mother was strict. She was very lenient with her son, and trusted him to be good at all times, which of course he was. There was one point, however, on which she was most insistent. Bost was never to play in the meadow near to their house, for it was well known that fairies would play there, and as everyone who lived at that time knew, no good will ever come of a human child playing with a fairy.

Of course, even the best behaved boy will forget his mother's warnings from time to time, and one fine summer's morning Bost looked out of his window and saw the meadow in all its glory. The grass was long and fine and the flowers were out, spreading a riot of red, purple, blue and yellow petals as far at the eye could see. Beautiful butterflies and bumble bees darted amongst the colour, and the whole scene swayed most seductively in the breeze. It was too good to resist, and Bost jumped out of bed and ran down to the meadow to play.

Bost's mother was in the kitchen when she looked out of the window and saw her son playing in the meadow. In alarm, she ran out of the house towards him, shouting at him to come back, but by the time she got to him he was nowhere to be seen. Frantically, she cast about for any sign of him, and saw something silver glinting at her from the spot where Bost had stood. She picked it up and looked at it more closely. It was a crumb of fairy bread. She looked up and saw, a little further away, another crumb. She walked to that and saw another beyond that, and another.

For the rest of that day Bost's mother followed the trail of silver crumbs as she became more and more frantic. It wasn't until the sun was beginning to go down that it led her to a large walled garden. This garden was well known to her, as indeed it was to all who lived nearby. It was the most beautiful garden there has ever been, and was surrounded by walls thirty feet high, with just a small gate in one side. It was owned by a jealous witch, who would never allow anyone to enter. Bost's mother hesitated; the witch was tremendously powerful, and there was no telling what she might do if she caught her in the garden. She was about to turn back and look elsewhere for her son, when she heard the unmistakable sound of Bost singing from over the high walls. Without a second's thought she pushed open the gate and ran inside.

She found herself in the most lovely place she had ever been. The imposing walls she had just passed through were hidden on the inside by tall hedges and trees. Glorious flower beds stretched on for miles, and roses bowed their heads to her as she passed. The garden hummed with all kinds of life. There was the cheerful chirping of small birds, the buzzing of bees, and huge butterflies sunned themselves lazily on the broad leaves of the plants that were at once everywhere, but never in your way. She could hear the faint tinkling of a stream in the distance, and she passed small ponds, each teeming with fish and good natured, ribbitting frogs. Bost's mother was overawed, and she quite forgot where she was until she turned and found herself face to face with the furious witch.

'What are you doing in my garden?' the witch asked, her face hard and cruel.

Bost's mother paled.

'I beg pardon. I know I shouldn't be here, but I'm looking for my son. He has been taken by the fairies some hours ago now, and I've been looking for him all day. I heard his voice in here, and I'm sure that he's in this garden somewhere. Please, I beg of you, let me find him. He's all the world to me.'

The witch hesitated.

'It may well be,' she said, 'that the fairies have taken your son here, for they often play in my garden. But I fear it's now too late for him. You people cannot stay for more that a few moments in the company of fairies before you become lost. I will let you stay here and search my garden if you wish, but I would counsel you to leave immediately. The touch of fairies isn't kind to humans.'

Bost's mother took the witch's hand in gratitude.

'You are wise, and I have no doubt that you speak sense, but I can't leave without finding my child. Losing him forever would be worse than anything that might happen to me at the hands of fairies.'

The witch nodded.

'Then good luck.'

And before Bost's mother could say another word the witch vanished into thin air.

Bost's mother searched for many hours in the garden, where it seemed to be perpetually bright with sunshine. She noticed that the sun had gone down outside the walls, but in the garden it was as bright as the most glorious summer's day. It was hot, and the heat became stifling. She sat down by a pond to catch her breath and to dip her feet in the cool water. She closed her eyes, and as she did so she felt a slight difference in the air around her. It was as if everything was much clearer. The water at her feet felt cooler, and somehow more delicious, and the sun on her back was warmer, and yet no longer stifling. It felt like velvet. She opened her eyes and saw, not far from her at all, Bost, playing with a group of fairy children.

With a cry of joy she ran to him and flung her arms around him, tears streaming down her face. The fairies ran off in alarm, hiding behind nearby bushes and trees. Bost turned to his mother, puzzled.

'What's the matter, mummy?'

Bost's mother looked up at the fairies around them. They were just children, like Bost, and seemed very shy. They peered at her curiously from behind leaves and hedges, and some even smiled nervously.

'Mummy, will you stay and play with us? My new friends don't have a mummy like I do. I think they'd like you.'

Bost's mother noticed for the first time that there was something different about her child. He seemed less clear than before, and she felt that she could almost see through parts of him. He was Bost, and yet was not Bost. Without another word to her Bost turned and started playing with the fairies again as if nothing had happened.

As she watched him, Bost's mother realised that he had been with the fairies for too long. It was only an echo of Bost that was now playing with them, nothing more. She wouldn't be able to take him back to the human world any more than you could take a shadow into a dark room. It was as if all she could now see of her son were his footprints on a beach or on a muddy riverbank, but the feet that had made them had long since passed. She also knew that if she stayed she too would fade away to an echo, and from that, to nothing at all. She looked at what was left of her son again, and he turned to her and smiled.

'Mummy, will you stay and play with us?'

Tears of hopelessness stung Bost's mother's eyes. She looked at the dark sky of the world outside the garden.

'My new friends don't have a mummy like I do. I think they'd like you.'

That was many years ago, and the walls of the garden are now long gone. The garden itself is overgrown and is no longer beautiful, but to this day if you stand in that same spot you can still hear the fairies playing. And if you listen very, very carefully, you can still faintly hear the echo of Bost's mother as she continues to sing lullabies to her long gone son, and the faintest trace of him still asks her if she'll stay and play with him and his fairy playmates.

A Warning to Art Lovers

In a place, neither near nor far, and a time, neither now nor then, lived a woman by the name of Mrs Marshall. And Mrs Marshall was a thief. Of course, I don't mean to say that she was an outlaw. She didn't rob banks or burgle houses or anything like that. No, Mrs Marshall was simply a dishonest woman who you wouldn't trust an inch with anything. I'm sure you know the type. The type that will borrow money with no intention of paying it back, or will lie to you just to get their own way, with no thought for anyone but themselves. The type that will take something whether they are entitled to it or not. Simply, a thoroughly unpleasant sort of a person.

It may surprise you to hear that Mrs Marshall had friends, and plenty of them in fact, for she was as charming as she was dishonest. One of her oldest and closest friends was a man by the name of Mr Austen. Mrs Marshall and Mr Austen had known each other for a very long time indeed, and saw each other most weeks, as they lived close to one another. Mr Austen valued Mrs Marshall's opinion very much, and would often ask her round to ask her advice on one thing or another. He respected her opinion so highly in fact, that when he discovered a number of what looked like expensive things in his attic that had belonged to his father he invited Mrs Marshall round immediately to see them and discuss what might be done with them.

Mrs Marshall didn't need to be asked twice, and before the day was out she found herself in Mr Austen's attic looking at a huge pile of expensive looking paintings, furniture and trinkets.

'I've always known all this was here,' Mr Austen explained, 'but I never realised quite how much there was. What do you think I should do with it all?'

Mrs Marshall rubbed her hands with glee. Some of these things must be worth a fortune!

'Well,' she began very slowly, 'I do so love furniture and paintings like this. If you wanted to get rid of them I would be more than happy to take one or two things off your hands. Those paintings, for example,' she said pointing to a pile of particularly fine oil paintings lying on the floor, 'would look beautiful in my house.'

'Oh no,' said Mr Austen, 'I could never part with these things. They belonged to my father after all; I couldn't give any of them away. I wanted to ask how you thought they might look best in my house.'

Mr Austen, as Mrs Marshall well knew, had been incredibly close to his father, and had never quite recovered from his sudden disappearance six years previously.

'Still,' Mrs Marshall pressed, picking up a fine oil lamp that lay next to the paintings, 'I was close to your father too, and I would dearly love something to remember him by. This lamp is exquisite, and not such a very big thing, do you thing I might be able to have just this to remember your father by?'

Not without some inward struggle, Mr Austen relented.

'Of course,' he told his friend, 'you may take that lamp in memory of my father, but please, no more. I couldn't bear to part with anything else of his.'

So saying he started to cry, and bent his head to search his pockets for a handkerchief while Mrs Marshall took up the lamp again in triumph. She was just popping the little thing in her pocket when she noticed a painting without a frame rolled up by the pile of pictures. She couldn't say why, but this painting immediately grabbed her interest, and she carefully took it and unrolled it to get a closer look at it.

It was quite an ordinary thing, just a picture of a house with a great big garden all around it. It was not unlike her own house in fact. She looked closer. It was expertly done, there was no doubt about that, and the more Mrs Marshall looked the more she felt that she must have this painting. To you or me I daresay that it would have looked like a plain old picture of a house, but if you would have asked Mrs Marshall she would have told you that it was like nothing she had ever seen before in her life.

She looked up and, seeing that Mr Austen was now engaged in poring over some old maps of this father's, she quickly rolled the painting back up and stuffed it up her shirt. Well, why not, she reasoned, her friend probably hadn't even seen it.

The rest of the day was spent in inspecting the remainder of the items in Mr Austen's attic, and if Mr Austen had noticed that the paining had gone he certainly didn't say anything. In triumph, Mrs Marshall made her way home at the end of the day with not only a new lamp but a new paining as well, both of which she intended to sell at a hefty price.

Mrs Marshall was extremely pleased with herself, and when she got home she unrolled the painting again to have a look at it. She loved it. In fact, she was so taken with it that she decided not to sell it as she had first planned, but to frame it and put it in her bedroom on the top floor of the house. She cleared a space on the wall opposite her bed and, finding that she already had a frame that fitted it just right, hung it there in pride of place. Once she had done so she stood for some time looking at it, quite in awe. Now that she had time to examine the picture a bit more closely she was struck even more by the skill of the painter. Put simply, it was the most realistic painting that Mrs Marshall had ever seen, and she almost felt as if she were gazing through a window rather than looking at a picture in a frame. The detail was incredible. She could even make out the individual bricks of the house, and fancied she could see the grass in the garden moving in a slight breeze that was playing about the scene. In fact, it seemed to her that the landscape looked different now to how it had appeared to her in Mr Austen's attic, and bore more than a passing resemblance to the countryside around her own house. Why, she even saw behind the house a tall, solitary ash tree that she hadn't noticed before, looking for all the world exactly like the one that stood behind her own home. The similarity was so striking that Mrs Marshall even ran to a window to look at the tree to make a full comparison. How extraordinary!

The next day another friend of Mrs Marshall's, a Mr Jones, came to dinner, and of course after dinner Mrs Marshall couldn't wait to take her friend up to her room and show him her new painting. Mr Jones was very impressed, and stood looking at the picture for quite some time.

'Well, what do you think?' asked Mrs Marshall. 'Isn't it wonderful?'

'It certainly is very skilfully done,' mused Mr Jones, his face now quite close to the picture. 'But I'm not sure if wonderful is the word I would use. The house and the landscape are all pretty enough, but I find this figure here a little disquieting, don't you?'

At this Mrs Marshall gave a start, for she certainly hadn't noticed any figure in the picture before now. She stepped closer to it and looked to where Mr Jones was pointing, and sure enough, at the bottom left hand corner of the picture there was indeed a figure. It was dressed all in black, with its head covered by a hood. It was the size and shape of a man, but seemed to be moving more like a frog or a spider, crawling towards the house. The only parts of it that she could see under its clothes were its hands, protruding from loose sleeves. These were abnormally white, with skin stretched tight over them. It was not at all a nice thing to look at.

To say that Mrs Marshall was taken aback would be an understatement; there is no question that the figure hadn't been there before. However, for fear of looking foolish she said nothing to Mr Jones, but rather agreed that yes, the figures wasn't to everyone's taste, but that it certainly was an interesting work, was it not? At this of course Mr Jones agreed, and Mrs Marshall hurried him away from the picture. Soon after this Mr Jones took his leave and returned to his own house for the night.

Mrs Marshall now kept a close eye on the painting, very interested to see what else might appear. She was sadly disappointed however, for there were no further additions to the scene. It did appear to her though, that over the coming days the crawling figure seemed to be getting closer to the house. The landscape seemed to be subtly changing as well, looking more and more like her garden with every day.

If Mrs Marshall had obtained the painting through honest means she may well have sought the advice of a friend, but as she didn't want the question of how she had come by it to come up she was forced to keep the matter to herself. Of course, she supposed she could still take it back to Mr Austen's, but she thought that ultimately it was silly to be scared of a painting, and resolved to leave it exactly where it was.

Whilst the painting was certainly a puzzle, Mrs Marshall had many other things to do besides watching a picture on her bedroom wall. It was the beginning of summer, and she found that the weather was quite warm enough for her to carry out a number of repairs to her house that she had been meaning to do for some time; patching a leak in the roof, weeding her garden, painting her front door and the like. She took a great deal of pride in her house, and these activities afforded her a lot of pleasure. She painted her front door a bright red, and liked the effect so much that she decided that she would also paint the window frames the same colour the next time she could afford to go into town and buy some more paint.

That night, as Mrs Marshall was going to bed she glanced at the painting, as she always did now, and stopped dead in her tracks. The front door of the house in the picture, which had been a dull brown, was now a bright red, just like hers. Mrs Marshall barely slept a wink that night.

The next day she took the painting off her wall, wrapped it up very carefully, and took it back to Mr Austen's house. She was quite prepared to accept whatever might happen to her, for the picture so troubled her now that the thought of having it in her house another night made her shudder.

But when she handed to painting over the Mr Austen and confessed all she was surprised by her friend's response.

'So you took the picture of the house?!' Mr Austen demanded, eyes blazing.

Full of contrition, Mrs Marshall unwrapped the painting and pleaded with Mr Austen to take it back, but he would have none of it.

'But this isn't it! Do you think you can fool me twice, once by stealing the painting and once again by trying to return another one in its place? You must think I'm an idiot! Get out!'

And without listening to another word Mrs Marshall could say her friend bundled her out of his house, trembling with rage and threatening much more severe action should she ever darken his doorstep again. Shaken, and without knowing what else to do, Mrs Marshall went back home and put the picture in a dark corner of her library, never meaning to uncover it again. But curiosity at what Mr Austen had said soon overcame her, and a few hours later she found herself coming back to it. Why had he not recognised it as his own? To be sure, the creeping figure was a new addition, as was the ash tree and the red front door, but it was still surely to be recognized as his original. In consternation she unwrapped it again to inspect it more closely.

The more she thought about, the more it did seem that the painting was indeed very different to the one she had stolen. The landscape and garden around the house had now changed so much that one would have been forgiven for thinking that whoever had painted it had set out to make a faithful copy of the countryside and garden around Mrs Marshall's house. And the house too had changed in a great many respects. The roof had become more rounded, and the number of chimneystacks had changed from one to two, just as there were on Mrs Marshall's house. She even fancied that through one of the top windows she could see a large vase on the windowsill, just like the one that stood in her own bedroom. That dreadful, crawling figure was closer still to the house, and noticing this such gave Mrs Marshall such a thrill of fear that she ran to the window, half expecting to see it making its way across her lawn. There was, of course, nothing there.

She decided that she wouldn't part with the painting after all, as she was curious to see how else it would change. And so she picked it and took it upstairs, hanging it once more in her bedroom.

It was a hot evening, and promised to be a warm, oppressive night, and Mrs Marshall was obliged to open a number of windows before sitting down to her supper. She dined early, and, quite tired out from the excitement of the day, decided to get an early night. Before going to bed she checked the painting once more and saw, with a shudder, that the hooded being now seemed to be right outside the house. She turned away quickly from the scene, so quickly that she failed to notice that something else had changed in the picture as well – a window on the ground floor of the house had been left open.

Unable to get to sleep, she read in bed for some time, unwilling to turn out the lights. It was the early hours of the morning before she finally felt that she could bear to make another attempt at sleeping, but before she did she took another look at the painting. She could have laughed out loud with relief, for she saw that the awful figure was gone! She scanned the picture anxiously to see if perhaps it was not climbing up the walls of the house like some dreadful spider, or lying lower in the grass, but there could be no doubt about it; it had vanished. Mrs Marshall was just about to clap her hands for joy when she noticed the open window.

Remembering that she had indeed left her library window open, Mrs Marshall flew downstairs and quickly closed it, running straight back up to the safety of her room, closing and locking the door behind her. She went straight back to the painting and saw that the downstairs window was now closed. More importantly though, that horrible figure was still nowhere to be seen.

She let out a sigh of relief, which was quickly curtailed by a sudden realisation.

'He's got in!' Mrs Marshall cried to herself, and turned back to the door in fright.

What she was going to do next I couldn't tell you, but one thing that is for certain is that she never got a chance to do it. As Mrs Marshall turned she heard a sudden dry rustling rush upon her, and all became as black as night as her ears were filled with a horrible, high pitched screaming.

A month after the disappearance of Mrs Marshall, when all attempts to find her had been abandoned, it fell to her friend Mr Jones to deal with her belongings, as Mrs Marshall had no family that could be found. Mr Jones knew little about art, and spent a day in Mrs Marshall's house packing up the collection of paintings that covered the walls, intending to sell them all as a job lot to the nearest gallery. One picture looked much like another to him, and he barely paid any of them a second glance as he wrapped them up and put them in boxes along with the rest of Mrs Marshall's things ready to be shipped out.

He had nearly finished for the day, and was in Mrs Marshall's bedroom, when he came across a painting that made him stop. He remembered it as the picture that Mrs Marshall had shown him when she had last seen him, with that horrible figure crawling towards the house. Mr Jones, as I say, didn't know much about art, but he could have sworn that the last time he saw the picture the figure had been crawling towards the house, not walking away from it, and he certainly hadn't been carrying anything. What was that, he wondered as he peered closer, that the hooded figure was bearing away from the house? He looked closer still, and realized with a shock that it was in fact the figure of a woman, limp in either death or a faint. She was wearing a nightgown, and the face, easily seen as the head lolled over a shoulder, was as pale as a ghost's. But the strangest thing, as Mr Jones would tell his friends later, was that if he hadn't known better and explained it away as the mistake of an overexcited mind, he would have sworn that the woman had looked exactly like Mrs Marshall.

Run with Us

Hill and vale do not meet, but people, as they move and drift about, will meet with many things. Some, much more than they have bargained for. This was the case for a man who lived many years ago, by the name of Griff. Griff was a timid man, and was gentle and kind, and he lived with his family in a small village on the edge of a thick forest. He loved his family very much, and doted on them, treasuring them more than anything else in the whole world, and his family returned his love a thousand fold. They were poor, but very happy.

One day, as he sometimes liked to do, Griff went for a stroll, venturing into the woods outside of his village. It was a peaceful morning, and he was very much enjoying himself, when suddenly he stumbled upon a group of trolls. Before he had time to even cry out they had fallen upon him, licking their lips and gnashing their teeth in delight. But they didn't eat him as he might have expected. Instead, they tied him up and sat looking at him, rolling their terrible eyes in confusion.

'What are you?' one of them said to him, drawing a little closer than the others.

Griff looked around at the terrible faces surrounding him as they watched him intently.

'I'm a man,' he said.

'A man!' they cried. 'What luck!'

And they all moved closer to him now, peering at him carefully.

'Tell us where to find more like you,' the biggest troll said to him. 'We're hungry, and we like to chew bones and munch flesh. We haven't seen one of your kind in a long time. Tell us where there are more like you, and we'll spare you, little man.'

'I can't do that,' said Griff. 'I won't betray my family and friends to you. Eat me if you must, but I won't help you to eat another person as long as I live.'

With that the troll gave a howl of anger, and reached out a huge, clawed hand to Griff's head.

'We shall see about that!' the troll cried.

Griff winced, expecting that his life would end at that moment, but he was surprised to find that the troll's touch, instead of striking him roughly, felt almost gentle. And now he felt somehow different. He opened his eyes to find that a terrible change had come over him. The ropes that had been binding him now lay broken on the floor, and as he looked down at his hands, he saw that they were huge and rough and green, exactly like the trolls'. He was suddenly filled with a fierce hunger, and he realised, as he looked at himself, that the trolls had turned him into one of them.

The big troll laughed triumphantly.

'Now we will go and feast, and we will soon see if you'll help us to eat other people, impudent man. Come,' he said, addressing them all, 'let's find a town and gorge, for there must be more like him somewhere!' and the trolls set off running at furious pace through the forest, smashing trees and tearing through bushes, and poor Griff found that he couldn't help but follow them.

They travelled like this for many days before finally they did indeed come across a town. The trolls instantly fell on it with whoops and cries of delight, and were soon smashing homes and bones and munching on the unfortunate inhabitants. Griff found that he wanted more than anything to join in with the carnage, for he was a troll now, and the hunger wouldn't leave him. But despite his growling stomach, as he saw his fellow trolls killing and crunching he felt a rage rise up within him. With a cry of fury he ran at them, but he hadn't got more than a few steps before he felt himself stopped as if by an invisible force. He stepped back, and ran at them again, but he couldn't get near the other trolls before his legs froze and his arms lost their power and hung limp at his sides. He tried again and again, but every time he made to run forward and stop the trolls his new body disobeyed him. He was a troll himself now, and unable to lift a finger against the others. In despair he sat miserably at the edge of the houses, watching the beasts destroy all before them, but he wouldn't take part in any of it. He imagined this happening to his own town, and to his own family, and he wept for the poor townsfolk.

And so the months passed. The trolls travelled through the countryside, destroying and eating any town or village they came across, and Griff went with them. He found himself as unable to leave his fellow trolls as he was to harm them. He would watch unhappily as they would smash and bash and crunch and munch any people they came across, but he would never take part. He survived by eating rocks and moss, although the taste of them made him sick, and they would never keep the terrible hunger from his belly for long.

He missed his family terribly, and hated what he had become. He didn't think things could get any worse until one day as they ran along he noticed that they were in a part of the woods that looked strangely familiar. As they tore through the undergrowth he realised that they were in the same woods where the trolls had caught him all those months ago, and they were in fact running towards his very village!

Fear clutched at Griff's human heart, but as a troll he couldn't stop running, the ever present hunger growing inside him. They burst forth from the trees still some way away from the village. He saw his old neighbours grab swords and pitchforks and spades, intent on defending themselves and their loved ones, but he knew it would be no use, for the trolls were unstoppable. In a moment the distance to the town had halved, and in another moment they were upon it. A great cry came up from both sides, one of delight and hunger from the trolls, and one of fear and dismay from the humans.

Griff saw his former friends and neighbours come at him to defend themselves, and he ran like a wounded animal away from the battle. Not knowing what else to do, he made for the poorest part of the village, where the houses were old and ramshackle and close together, and came to his old house. All was quiet there. As softly as he could, Griff crept up to a window and peered inside. There he saw his trembling wife sitting under the kitchen table, clutching their crying children. In agony Griff turned away and sunk to his knees under the window, putting his troll head in his hands.

For the first time troll tears sprang from his eyes, running onto his sharp talons. In frustration he clawed at himself, raking his hands across his tough, leathery hide. It was then that he felt something that he hadn't felt since he had met the trolls – he felt a scratch.

Griff looked down at where he had clawed at himself and saw that one of his talons had cut deeper than the rest, and had in fact scored a long, deep line across his chest. Curious, he put a claw into the scratch, bit his lip, and pulled deeper. He was amazed to see that if he scratched deep enough his troll skin would peel away like the skin of a banana. Excitedly, Griff set about clawing as hard as he could at himself with both hands. The pain was intense, but he wasn't to be deterred, and he scratched and scratched until there lay at his feet the skin of a whole troll. Griff couldn't believe what he saw. He was free! Cautiously, he raised his hands to his face to feel his old human skin as he remembered, but instead of a soft, familiar face he still felt the tough, detestable hide of a troll. In horror, Griff looked down at himself to see that he was still just as much a troll as before.

From the centre of town he heard the screams of his former friends as they fought the trolls, and the anger rose up in him once more. He tore at himself again, deeper this time, bringing tears of pain to his eyes. He tore off another, and another, and then another layer of troll skin, each one more painful than the last, until five layers lay at his feet and still he was a troll.

By now Griff felt like his whole body was aflame, and as his claws ripped away at his skin for the sixth time he knew that he wouldn't be able to do it for a seventh. When the job was done he collapsed, more dead than alive, falling onto the pile of skins by his side.

He didn't lie for long. The screams and shouts and the trolls' triumphant munching and crunching were closer now, and they woke Griff with a start. He felt different. Trembling, he raised a hand to his face, and saw instead of a huge, gnarled troll's hand his own slim, pink, very human, hand. He reached up to his cheek, and this time felt not the hard, unforgiving skin of a troll, but the warm, tender skin of his own face. Griff shouted for joy. This time he really was free! More cries came from even closer this time, and he wheeled around, full of determination. He ran into his house and up to his room, moving so quickly he didn't know whether his wife had seen him or not. There he found his old clothes and hurriedly dressed himself. He left the house again running in the direction of the screams, picking up a sword that had fallen as he did so.

I believe that there is no one who has ever seen anyone fight trolls as Griff did that day. The trolls were laughing and gobbling up everyone that they saw, but they stopped, amazed, when they saw Griff. Without a pause he ran at the nearest one and stabbed his sword with all his might deep into its impenetrable hide. To everyone's amazement the sword broke the skin and found the troll's black heart. No sooner had it died then Griff had moved onto the next one, dispatching it with similar ease. The remaining trolls now gathered around him, roars of anger issuing from their bloody lips, but Griff was too quick for them. He stepped aside as they lunged for him and stabbed again and again, until only the biggest troll was left. The troll laughed at him.

'Put aside your puny sword,' he said. 'I can just as easily undo what you've done, you wretch,' and with that it stretched out a claw to Griff's head once more.

But Griff was not the same timid man who had been first transformed in the woods. With a troll's rage and strength in his heart he raised his sword and brought it down with all his might onto the reaching claw, cutting it clean off. With a cry of pain the troll withdrew its hand, but it wasn't quick enough, and soon it too lay in the mud with Griff's sword deep in its heart.

The townsfolk could scarce believe their eyes. Here before them stood a man who had just killed five trolls with just a sword and his bare hands, and not only that, it was gentle Griff, the man who wouldn't hurt a fly, who they thought they had lost months ago! A mighty cheer went up, and all wept for joy. Griff's wife and children, who had long thought him dead, ran to him, and he held them to him as if his life depended on it. Indeed, he hugged his youngest daughter so tight that she cried out in pain.

For Griff had not been left unchanged by his time as a troll. The once timid, weak man was now as strong as an ox and brave as a lion. He helped his neighbours to rebuild their homes, holding up whole houses by himself. He found that he no longer jumped at shadows, and didn't even tremble at the memory of fighting the trolls. He now carried a sword with him everywhere he went.

The troll carcasses were huge, and only Griff had the power to move them from where they lay in the middle of the town. He dragged them by their feet, two at a time, far out beyond the village walls and into the forest. He'd just taken the last one there, and was about to go home when something caught his eye. Where his sword had pierced the skin of one of the trolls he thought he saw a glimmer of something pink underneath, instead of the dark green of a troll's skin.

Intrigued, he took his sword and cut into the body, widening the wound. He gave a gasp, and then continued to cut at the dead troll with renewed vigour. He then moved onto the next one, and then the next, and then the next, amazed at what he saw.

When Griff had finished he had cut away all the skin from each troll, and before him lay the bodies of five very ordinary looking men and women, just like him . But what struck him most was the look on their faces. Every single one of them wore a look of intense sadness. They were the faces, Griff would later tell his wife, of prisoners, and he hadn't felt more sorry for anyone in all his life.

Wishing Well

Everyone knows the tall well that stands by itself in the empty town of Dalles. It's a beautiful thing, made of precious stones and a full twenty feet tall, covered with the most exquisite carvings. There are hunting scenes on it, and scenes of great battles, of kings and queens, of knights fighting dragons, weddings, festivals and all manner of things, all carved so skilfully that you would believe that the figures were living and breathing. Life shines out of them, and so real do they look that if you were to touch one of these figures you would be half surprised to find that it wasn't warm to the touch. The well is full of water, yet the town around it is empty. In fact, it is the well itself, with its gay, joyful scenes and blindly smiling faces, that has brought about the downfall of the once thriving Dalles.

It was built in the days when Dalles was a rich and successful town. Dalles had grown over the years from a small village to a centre of trade for the local area, and people would come from many miles away to buy and sell at the market there. Life was good, and the mayor was proud of his town. But, not content with this, he wanted it to be famous throughout the land.

'What we need,' he said to his ministers one day, 'is a monument to this town's brilliance. Something extraordinary, something so fantastic that people will flock to Dalles just to see it, and will talk about us from East to West and North to South and back again. We need something beautiful. Send for The Carver.'

The Carver was a local man by the name of Robert Stoneman. He was a great artist, and his skill at statuary was known far and wide. Wherever men spoke of him he was known as Robert the Carver, or simply, The Carver. He was a favourite of the mayor's, and well liked in the town.

The Carver was duly sent for, and he came and met with the mayor of Dalles, and the mayor said to him;

'Carver, this town needs your skill. At the centre of Dalles I want you to build something great. Something that will make this town famous. I want your finest work, Carver. Spare no expense. Every material and tool you ask for will be made available to you. As much help as you want shall be yours. Take as long as you need, for this shall be your crowning achievement. I will pay whatever you ask, and pay it gladly, for the price of glory can never be too high.'

And so Robert the Carver set to work. Following what the mayor had said he went right to the centre of Dalles, and there he saw a dusty old well in the town square, crumbling and green with neglect. He ordered men to dig a new well next to it, and at this site he announced he would set to work. He ordered tonnes upon tonnes of the finest pink marble, jade, agate, onyx and rock crystal. He ordered the best tools money could buy, and sent for the very best men to help him. Still he wasn't satisfied. He ordered carnelian and alabaster and gems, and it wasn't until even the mayor was beginning to become alarmed by his lengthy demands that he finally stopped, and began to carve.

For years The Carver and his team toiled under a huge tent in the centre of Dalles while the townsfolk drew their water from the small, ugly well nearby. None could see how the new well was progressing, and The Carver never said a word about it in all that time. What on earth could be going on behind that tent? The locals had no answer for each other. Even The Carver's team were sworn to silence and wouldn't be drawn. The works went on for so long that they became a spectacle in themselves, and people would come to gawp and wonder at what was going on behind the mysterious awnings. For a whole generation no one was any the wiser. And then, finally, after thirty years, The Carver announced that he had finished.

Immediately people started to gather to see what on earth Robert Stoneman had been building for all that time under his mysterious tent. Merchants left their shops, children played truant from school, and the local council adjourned all meetings so that all could see just what The Carver had made for the town of Dalles. Soon, the town square was full with curious onlookers. At last, with the huge crowd gathered around him, Robert removed the tent, revealing the fruits of his long labours to the incredulous town.

The mayor hadn't been wrong when he had told Robert that this would be his crowning achievement. In the centre of Dalles he had built a well of such breathtaking beauty that words failed all who saw it. It was a masterpiece, the like of which the world had never seen. Statues so lifelike that they seemed to have jumped out of the very water danced and hunted and revelled around it, carved from warm pink marble, with sparkling jewels for eyes that twinkled outwards mischievously. Strange animals from half remembered myths and long forgotten legends weaved their way through, up and over the scenes, twisting their bodies sinuously and baring their polished teeth at all who dared to look at them. More familiar animals – peacocks with fans of emeralds and rubies, lions with claws of diamond, and deer with amethyst hooves gambled and preened about it all, while gargantuan fish raced below in a sea of polished sapphire. Above everything a jade bucket hung on a rope shot through with gold, lowered into cool, crystal clear water by the turn of a handle made of polished agate of red, blue and orange. Even the birds in their trees nearby had stopped their singing in amazement at what they saw.

It was a triumph, and the mayor and the whole town of Dalles were delighted with their new well. Everything happened just as the mayor had said it would; Dalles became famous overnight, and people came from far and wide to look at the famous well made by Robert the Carver, and talked about it from East to West and North to South and back again. The town and mayor became rich from all these new visitors. Businesses all over Dalles boomed, and The Carver was given a palatial house in the best part of town as a thank you. He was honoured wherever he went, and became Dalles' favourite son.

But people are fickle, and not a year had gone by before the residents of Dalles began to whisper to each other about The Carver. They were worried. If Robert the Carver had made them such a fantastic well, then what was to stop him from going to another town and building an even better one? Then no one would care for their well anymore. They had got used to their fame and their riches, and the idea of becoming second best was far more than they could stomach.

And so the people went to the mayor and they whispered, quietly, slyly, in his ear. They asked him to kill The Carver. The mayor was shocked at such a thought, and told the people that he would do no such thing. He sent them away again, repulsed at what they asked of him. But the people had planted the seed of suspicion in his head, and slowly that suspicion grew. It was true, he had to admit, that if Robert the Carver did go to another town and build a better well then no one would look twice at his beloved Dalles again. Just like his fellow townsfolk, he had grown accustomed to the life the well had brought him, and the idea of losing it left him very uneasy indeed.

The idea of killing Robert was not an easy one to swallow, but still, the idea that something must be done would not leave the mayor. And so he invited The Carver to a party he knew he would attend - a party to celebrate his genius. Robert was flattered, and gladly went, for who would miss a party like that?

But this was to be no ordinary party. As soon as The Carver arrived the mayor ordered his men to hold him and bind him. This they did, and they then took him to the town dungeons. There they put out his eyes so that never again would he carve anything of beauty, and cut out his tongue so that he would never be able to direct the building of such a wonderful well again. Then they led him home in this pitiable state, where his apprentice received him in shock.

And thus the people of Dalles were satisfied, and the mayor rested easy in his bed once more. The visitors continued to pour in, and business kept booming, and all continued in Dalles just as it had done.

But The Carver didn't forget what had been done to him. Many weeks later, when his apprentice had nursed him back to health, Robert instructed the young man to lead him to his well at the dead of night. The warm marble still sang to him in the blackness, and he knew where the dark, still waters were even without his sight. Standing on the edge of the well he cursed it with his absent tongue, promising that just as it had once brought riches and life to Dalles, it would now bring only the town's destruction. The famous statues grinned back at his unseeing eyes in silent agreement.

And then, before his horrified apprentice, Robert the Carver threw himself into the well, where he drowned without a struggle. From that day on the waters of the famous well at Dalles have been foul, and all who have drunk from it have died. In vain the residents of the town dug another well, then another, then another, but all water that they drew was death. The residents were forced to leave, and no one visited anymore. Dalles fell into disuse and disrepair, and now there's nothing left standing save for a few ruined houses and Robert's marvellous well, now a fabulous tomb for the man who created such a wonder.

The Queen of Shadows

There was once a woman who lived all by herself in a room that had no doors or windows in the middle of a mountain. The walls of her room were made of stone, and were very high, higher than she could ever climb. At the top of them there was half a roof to let the sun in during day and the moon at night, but she had shelter from the rain and the snow. It was warm and cosy in her little room, and she had everything that she could ever need. There was a large, comfortable bed, with a thick, feather down mattress and many blankets and pillows. There was a fireplace with an ample supply of wood for when it got too cold, and a large heavy oak table in the room that was always covered with every kind of delicious food that you could imagine, for no matter how much the woman ate, when she woke the next day she would discover that the table had been replenished with another banquet just for her.

The woman was perfectly happy; she had grown up in this room without ever seeing another soul. She couldn't remember her mother or her father, and she never thought to wonder where her endless supply of food came from, or her bed or the wood for her fire. She would spend her days sitting and eating, watching shadows cast by the sun on the walls of her room. These shadows were everything to her. She would make up long, beautiful songs about them that she would sing, and at night she would watch the different, flickering shadows cast by her fire, singing songs about those as well until she fell asleep. She had no idea that there was a world beyond her room, and to her the shadows that she saw on her walls were as real and important as any solid, living thing might be to anyone else in the outside world.

She had no idea, that is, until one day a little fairy appeared in her room. The woman was sitting at her big table eating when the fairy appeared and said to her, 'You really shouldn't eat so much you know.'

'Well,' said the woman, so surprised that she stopped chewing for a second, 'a talking shadow, and one with colour!'

'I'm not a shadow,' said the fairy. 'I'm a fairy. And you shouldn't eat so much because you're being fattened up to eat.'

At this the woman put her food down. Her jaw dropped.

'Why should I believe you?' the woman asked. 'Why are you telling me this?'

'It's rather a long story,' said the fairy, 'and I haven't much time. We fairies can't make ourselves visible to your kind for long. But it's a story you need to hear. I'll go as quick as I can so please try to pay attention.'

And the fairy sat down delicately on the table between a plate of rolls and a leg of ham and proceeded to tell his tale.

'Many years ago now, when I was a young fairy, and much smaller than I am now, I was foolish enough to get caught in a spider's web.'

'Pardon me,' said the woman, 'but what's a spider's web?'

The fairy pointed to a spider's web in the corner of the woman's room.

'You see that beautiful silken net in the corner there? That's a spider's web. And the handsome eight legged creature in the middle of it is the spider. He catches whatever flies into his web and eats it, including fairies if they're stupid enough.'

'But Fairy,' said the woman 'I don't think that can ever have happened, for I have seen the spider's web since the spider made it many weeks ago now, and I haven't seen you fly into it. In fact I don't think I've ever seen you before in my life.'

At this the fairy looked at the woman.

'What if there was more than one spider's web?' he asked.

'But you can see for yourself,' the woman protested, 'there is not.'

'There is a world,' the fairy told her, 'outside of this room. And in that world there are a great many spiders' webs, and many things that you have never seen before. Out there,' he said, pointing upwards, 'lies the kingdom of Dain.'

'What is a kingdom?' the woman asked.

The fairy thought for a minute.

'It's like a room,' he said finally, 'only much bigger.'

'How much bigger?'

'Well,' said the fairy, 'it's as big as the king wants to make it. He rules the kingdom.

'And what's a world?' the woman asked.

'The world is the place where the light gets in,' the fairy said. 'A world is even bigger than a kingdom. There are many kingdoms in a world.'

'And who rules that?' the woman asked, quite sensibly.

'Well, no one person,' the fairy answered.

'And how big is this world?' the woman persisted.

'The world is different sizes to different people,' the fairy told him. 'The only limit to it is how much you know about it. Now please,' he continued, 'let me carry on with my story. There will be many things in it that you don't understand yet, but you will in time, don't interrupt again.'

The woman stayed silent and nodded.

'As I was saying,' went on the fairy, 'once, many years ago when I was much smaller I got myself stuck in a spider's web. Now, the spider that lived in the web would have eaten me if it hadn't been for a beautiful young woman who was walking past at the time and heard my cries for help. She took pity on me and carefully untied me, setting me free.

Some time later the king of Dain decided that his son should marry. His son was an extraordinarily handsome youth, and as the king was very vain he decided that his son should marry a woman equally as beautiful. And so he held a beauty contest, and invited all the women from his kingdom to take part. He chose the birds of his kingdom to be the judges, for with their bright feathers and lovely singing voices there are no better judges of beauty. And so they all lined up on a tree outside the palace as the suitors came. Elves and witches and fairies and many others came in the hope of winning the king's son, but there were none were so lovely in all the land as the beautiful young woman with the kind heart who had saved my life, who happened to be a simple fisherman's daughter.

She was chosen to marry the prince and there was much rejoicing, but not everyone was happy with this decision. A beautiful young witch called Evslin had also hoped to marry the prince, and when she was beaten she was outraged. She vowed vengeance then and there on the prince and his new bride to be.

Without delay the royal couple were married, and lived very happily for a year. But when the princess bore the prince a daughter the witch took her revenge. She spirited the daughter away and gave her to a man eating giant, who put her in a room with no doors or windows in the middle of a mountain. The giant keeps her there, feeding her every day, fattening her up to one day eat her. The baby is a grown woman now, and the time has come for her to be eaten. That woman is you. You are a Princess of Dain, and your name is Bernar.'

Bernar was aghast.

'But what can I do?' she asked in a panic. 'I don't want to be eaten!'

'Your mother saved my life once,' said the fairy, 'and so I will save yours. If you do as I say your life will be spared.'

And so saying he flew right up to the roof of the Bernar's room, and let fall one end of a long, silken rope down to the surprised prisoner below while he tied the other end to an outcrop of rock on the room's ceiling.

'Climb up the rope!' the fairy called. 'Quickly, there isn't much time!'

Bernar wasted no time, but took hold of the end of the rope with both hands and began to climb for all she was worth. She had spent her whole life in between four walls, doing nothing but eat, and she had certainly never climbed a rope before. The going was slow and hard and the rope was long, but after a great deal of effort and words of encouragement by the fairy she finally managed to reach the top of her prison and climb up into the open air of the world outside.

But nothing had prepared Bernar for the wide expanse of the world in all its glory. She felt the wind blowing on her for the first time, making her cold, and her eyes hurt, unused as they were to seeing things under direct sunlight. She looked about her desperately and called out for the fairy, but she couldn't see him anywhere; he had quite disappeared. Bernar felt faint from all the new sights and smells and sounds assailing her. She looked up to see what was making everything so bright, and saw, for the first time not hidden behind a stone roof, the sun, shining down upon her. She had never seen anything like it, and stood transfixed, unable to tear her eyes away from this disc of fire above her. But no one had ever told Bernar not to look directly at the sun, and she soon found that her eyes began to hurt and her vision to fade. In alarm, she looked away at last from the sky but it was too late. Darkness covered Bernar's eyes. She took a hesitant step forward and fell down the mountain.

When Benar woke again she didn't know what to do. She still couldn't see, and was as helpless as the smallest infant. She stumbled blindly about this way and that, never getting more than a few feet before she tripped and fell. Though she couldn't know it, she was on a mountainside far above the magnificent royal palace of Dain, and over the days her stumbling brought her first closer, and then further away from, but never within sight of, the castle.

Bernar had grown fat in the giant's prison, and so didn't mind so much that she couldn't eat as she sightlessly wandered the mountainside, for she had no reason to be hungry. Every time she fell into a river or stream she would drink from it, and when she judged it to be night she would lie and sing songs of her shadows to herself until she fell asleep.

It was in this pitiable condition that one of the king's gardeners, out in the country gathering rare flowers for the royal garden, found her. Bernar was sitting on the banks of a stream and singing such a wonderful song that at first the gardener was afraid, thinking that it was a witch that he had disturbed. But Bernar looked so dishevelled and sad that the gardener decided that this could not be.

'Hello there,' he said, startling Bernar.

'Who's there?' Bernar asked quickly, looking about her in fear.

'Please don't worry, I don't mean to hurt you,' said the gardener. 'Can't you see me?'

'I can't,' said Bernar. 'Please help me, for I've been blinded by a gold plate that sits in the sky, and I can't find any table to eat from. I don't know where I am, and I'm sure that I'll start to starve before long.'

And poor Bernar proceeded to tell the gardener everything that had led her to that moment, but for one thing. In her unhappy state she couldn't remember the name of the kingdom the fairy had said that her parents ruled. The gardener, for his part, was a newcomer to the land, and could never have guessed that his master and mistress were the king and queen in the unhappy woman's tale. Nevertheless, he took poor Bernar and led her back to the palace to be fed and looked after.

It wasn't long before news of this stranger spread round the palace. And not long after that before the story of a strange blind woman reached the king and queen. Peeved, the king sent for the gardener.

'Tell me,' the king asked the gardener, 'what right have you to bring this woman into our palace? To feed her with our food, let her drink our wine and sleep in one of our beds? What right have you at all?'

'I have none, I know, your majesty,' the gardener answered, 'but this woman can sing the most beautiful songs I have ever heard.

Songs all of her own devising, and lovelier than the loveliest hymns ever sung in this hall.'

This didn't impress the king one bit, but the queen, who was a great lover of music, said to the gardener,

'Then bring her before us, and we shall judge for ourselves whether or not her singing makes her worthy of our generosity.'

And so Bernar was brought before the king and queen and told to sing. She was shy at first, but encouraged by the gardener she began, very quietly at first, and then louder and louder. She sang of her world of shadows, of how they flickered and danced, rose and fell, merged and twisted and twined and above all, of how real they were. She sang of them as if they were home. As her voice reached through the palace all who heard it stopped what they were doing to listen, for the gardener had been right, it was a song of unequalled beauty.

After she had finished no one spoke. All were too stunned by this otherworldly singer in front of them to speak.

Confused, Bernar turned to the gardener at her side, who stood with eyes glistening with tears, and asked,

'Was that alright?'

"My child,' said the queen, descending from her throne, 'you have the most wonderful voice I have ever heard. Your friend here is moved to tears, and my husband sits speechless with amazement. Pray tell me, where did you learn to sing like that, and how did you come to be here?'

'Oh,' Bernar said, 'no one taught me.'

And she told the queen her story, exactly as she had told it to the gardener. The queen listened with growing amazement, and at the end asked her,

'And did the fairy tell you the name of your parent's kingdom?'

'She did,' Bernar admitted, but I can't remember what it is.'

The king gave a start on his throne.

'Was it by any chance,' he asked in a trembling voice, 'Dain?'

'Yes!' exclaimed Bernar, 'That's it!'

'My daughter!' the queen cried, embracing Bernar and crying for joy.

She held Bernar so tightly she felt that she could barely breathe, and peppered her with a thousand kisses, And when her tears of joy at seeing her daughter once more fell upon Bernar's sightless eyes, the princess found that she could see again, and the first thing she saw was the face of her mother that she had never known.

A happier reunion there never was. The king leapt down from his throne and threw his arms around his wife and his daughter. The queen gave the order that a huge celebration was to be held in the great hall of the palace that night, and the whole kingdom was invited. Singing and rejoicing were to be heard throughout the land of Dain, for the princess that everyone had thought was dead had returned.

A huge feast was held, with Bernar in the place of honour, sitting between her two parents. She had never been happier in her whole life. It was a long night, full of laughter and smiles and tears of joy, and it was some time before anyone noticed that a beautiful witch had appeared in their midst, looking at Bernar and her parents with terrible hatred.

'You!' Evslin exclaimed as they hall grew silent around her, pointing her finger at the queen, 'You will pay for this!'

And before anyone could say anything she turned into a huge black bird, terrible to see, and with eyes blazing flew from the hall. She flew back to the mountain where Bernar had been kept prisoner for all those years, for the giant who had kept her was the witch's son. She told him to destroy the kingdom of Dain for the terrible wrong that the queen had done to her. And he did not fail to obey.

The giant raged down from his mountain, laying waste to all within his grasp. Farmers tried to stop him with their pitchforks and hoes but they were brushed aside like twigs. Blacksmiths tried to fight him with their huge hammers and sharp tongs but he trod them into the ground. Fish sellers, potters, butchers and bakers all tried to fight him off but the giant seemed to be invulnerable. The palace guard were dispatched to defend the realm but they soon found themselves scattered like matchstick men. No one could stop the giant, and it seemed clear that soon the kingdom of Dain would be nothing more than rubble and dust.

It was in the midst of all this calamity, when the giant could be seen from the palace windows smashing his way through the town towards them, that the fairy appeared once more to Bernar.

'Oh, Fairy,' Bernar cried, 'Please say that you have appeared to help me again! Whatever is to be done? Soon my parents and I will be smashed to smithereens! No one can stop the giant. Oh! What can we do?'

'Do not worry,' said the fairy. 'I will tell you if you listen very carefully. The giant has but one weak spot. When he was very young his mother covered him with an enchantment that makes him invincible to all that he does not fear. Nothing can hurt him the he isn't afraid of. But there is nothing that scares a giant more than his own shadow.'

'But that's ridiculous!' Bernar cried. 'How can his own shadow possibly hurt him? Shadows don't hurt anyone!'

But the fairy had vanished once more.

Finding herself alone, Bernar rushed out onto the castle battlements. She could see before her, in the midst of his devastation, the giant striding towards her. It was late afternoon, and the sun was low in the sky, and Bernar could see that the giant cast a long shadow behind him as he walked. More men rushed at the giant, but he brushed them aside as if they had been mere ants. His progress seemed unstoppable.

Alone on the battlements, Bernar did the only thing she knew how to do; she sang. She sang of the power and majesty of the giant's shadow that now stood before her, the biggest she had ever seen. She sang of its beauty, so different to that of its owner, and of its wondrous depths. Her song was so magical that the men fighting, far below at her feet, began to cry, and it even reached the ears of the murderous giant as he drew near. He paused for a second, and cocked his ear to listen to this sublime music.

'That's a very pretty song,' he said, 'but what a stupid thing to sing about. My shadow! Pah! If you're thinking that it'll sway my heart then you're quite wrong, it'll take for more than silly singing like that to stop the likes of me!'

And so saying he stepped forward with a step that was to bring him within reach of the castle. Terrified as she was, Bernar continued to sing, and as she did so she saw that the giant was brought up short just as he was reaching for her by something tugging hard on the hem of his cloak.

Amazed that anyone should have the nerve, much less the strength, to do such a thing, the giant turned, but saw only his shadow standing behind him. It was much bigger than him and

132

black, blacker than the darkest night. Terror struck the giant's heart, and for a second he stood stock still, paralysed with fear. But he soon mastered himself and turned once more back towards the castle. And still Bernar kept singing.

Again the giant reached for the princess, and again he felt a hard tugging at the hem of his cloak as he did so. Once more he wheeled around but saw only his shadow, even bigger now, behind him, and once more fear chilled him to his core.

But the giant was not a brute to be stopped, and so he turned back to the castle and the still singing Bernar a third time. But this time he didn't even have time to raise his hand to the castle before the tugging, harder now than ever, stopped him again. For a final time he wheeled around, and saw nothing but his shadow, bigger than he had ever seen it before, standing behind him. A horror for the darkness at his feet took hold of him, and he found that he could not move. So scared was he that he didn't even notice that Bernar had finally stopped singing to pick up a huge spear and hurl it at him. The spear passed through his neck, killing him instantly, and he fell into the welcoming arms of his silhouette.

And that is how the kingdom of Dain was saved. At once, the fairy appeared again, laughing for joy, a great cheer went up from the ruins of the town, and the king and queen rushed out onto the battlements to congratulate their brave daughter. Only Bernar remained sombre.

'What's wrong?' asked the fairy. 'You've slain the giant! Why do you not smile?'

'But the witch is not dead,' Bernar replied. 'She will return again, surely.'

'I think not,' laughed the fairy. 'She has fled! I should be very surprised if you hear from her again as long as you live.'

And neither the princess, nor anyone else, did live to see the fairy so surprised, for Evslin never did bother Dain again. The town was slowly rebuilt, and Bernar went on to live a happy life with her parents, and made a very just ruler when they had died. Some say that she was the wisest queen Dain has ever known, for when someone knows that even something's shadow has a value, they will consider nothing to be worthless.

Death's Flower

I do not really mean that this story is true, but it is certainly not a lie.

As is well known, our world is made up of two vast kingdoms, the Kingdom of the Living, and the Kingdom of the Dead. The Kingdom of the Dead is a limitless place, ruled over by Death, where it's always night and never day. The Kingdom of the Living, of course, has no one ruler, and for a long time was far more full than the Kingdom of the Dead, for Death in not by nature a greedy ruler. For a great many years, in fact, Death's kingdom was mostly empty. In the middle of it stands a gigantic mountain, taller than any mountain we have here in the land of the living. At the top of this mountain there once grew a single white flower that could give everlasting life to whoever ate it. Of course, such a prize is of no consequence to those who have already died, and so the lonely flower stood at the top of its mountain for thousands of years, with no one ever lifting a finger to disturb it.

But eventually news of the flower managed to reach the Kingdom of the Living. There too, it was many years before anyone so much as even thought about it. Although a few people made the trip to Death's kingdom each year, no one had ever made the return trip back to the land of the living, so what use could the flower possibly be to anyone?

But one day a young man by the name of Yorke got to hear of the flower. Yorke was a poor man, and lived in a small village with his young daughter whom he loved more than all the world. A terrible sickness had taken hold of her, and she was dying. No doctors could help her, and Yorke was at his wits' end. In his desperation he decided that the flower was the only thing that could save her. He determined to travel to the Kingdom of the Dead and to take the flower and bring it back to her. When he told her of his plan she cried out in fear, but he assured her that he wouldn't be gone for longer than a few days. Leaving a neighbour by her side to tend to her, that night he set off on his impossible quest.

He travelled for a day and a night to the unguarded crack in the centre of the earth that was the doorway to the land of the dead, and unseen by anyone, he slipped inside.

Once there he made straight for the mountain, taking care to take whatever back roads he could. It was so very dark in there, but he knew better than to strike a light, for that would mark him out as a living man, and so he felt his way through the cold, perpetual night.

In this way Yorke managed to travel almost completely unnoticed through the Kingdom of the Dead. But unknown to him, he had been watched from the moment he had set foot in that dismal land by Morphia, Death's daughter, and princess of the kingdom. Nothing ever escaped her notice, and she watched and followed in fascination as this impudent young man made his way across her realm. She had never seen a living thing before, and Yorke was like nothing she had ever come across. Even in the pale light of the deathly moon his golden hair shone, and his cheeks glowed with a life she had never known. As Morphia spied on this strange creature she found herself falling in love. Finally, she could bear it no longer, and at the foot of the mountain she confronted him.

'Mortal,' she said, appearing before him suddenly from the shadows, 'what brings you here, to my kingdom?'

Yorke started. A moment ago there had been nothing before him but darkness, and now in front of him stood a woman as pale and as thin as bone, with raven black hair and eyes like coals. He knew at once that it must be Death's daughter who addressed him, and his knees trembled at the thought.

'Please, your highness,' he began, 'I seek only the flower that grows atop this mountain, for, as you know, it will convey everlasting life upon whoever eats it. Indeed, no one in this kingdom has any use for it, as the dead have no life to prolong. But my daughter in the Land of the Living is dying, and only this flower can save her. Please, let me take it to her. Her life means more to me than I can ever say.'

As Yorke spoke, Morphia was transfixed. She stood in silence, unable to speak for the beauty of him. Yorke stood too, silent and in fear.

For the first time the Princess of the Dead felt her heart melt, and she resolved to help this poor young man if she could.

'You will never make it to the flower,' she said, 'and in failing, you will suffer a face worse than the death you fear for your daughter. The flower is surrounded by great vines that are covered by thorns. These thorns are many and they are sharp, there is no way for a mortal to pass them without being scratched a millions times over.'

But Yorke was undeterred.

'I will take my chances with mere thorns, your highness,' he said. 'We have them in my land too.'

'Not like this,' Morphia continued. 'There are two types of thorns. The first type you must make your way through will add time to your life, a year for every scratch.'

'So much the better then,' said Yorke. 'I would surely welcome as many extra years as I could get.'

'And I would agree with you,' said the princess, 'were in not for the second type of thorn. The second type confers a deep, terrible pain that will not end for the rest of your life. A pain that is unbearable, but will not kill you. These thorns will tear at you so much that you will have to stop before you reach your goal, but by then you will have been scratched by as many thorns of the first type, and you will be condemned to live for an eternity in the most unimaginable agony. It's a certain fate, I assure you.'

'But,' Morphia went on, 'I could fetch this flower for you. I am able to change my shape, to fly between the vines and avoid the thorns and their scratches. The only thing I ask in return is that you allow me to accompany you back to the Kingdom of the Living, and once there, to marry me.'

To such an offer Yorke readily accepted. Morphia lost no time in flitting up the mountain and bringing the flower back to him. She then showed him the quickest way back across her kingdom, cloaking him in her own personal darkness so that he wouldn't be seen by anyone, not even Death himself. They passed back out through the crack that separates the Kingdoms of the Living and the Dead, and together they stepped, blinking, into the land of life.

Immediately Morphia turned to Yorke.

'I have kept my end of the bargain, and now you must keep yours. You must marry me today.'

'I will keep my promise,' Yorke said, 'But first we must return to my daughter and give her this flower so that I can save her life. Then I will marry you as I swore, your highness.'

And so the two travelled for a day and a night back to Yorke's village, to bring aid to his dying child. But when they arrived, Yorke found that things were not as they had been.

The thriving village that he had left just a few days earlier was now empty and abandoned. Many of the buildings were not as he remembered, and those that were he found were deserted and crumbling. In alarm, he hurried through the empty streets to his house, but when he got to where it had been he found nothing more than ruins, with weeds and tangled vines choking what remained of the house that had once stood there. With a cry Yorke fell to his knees and with his bare hands dug desperately at the crumbled masonry and dirt, calling out his daughter's name at the top of his voice, but no one answered. He found nothing. Eventually he rose once more with tears streaming down his face and hands bloody and torn. He began to wander, lost and dazed, through the abandoned village, calling out for his daughter. But no one answered, and no one came.

What Yorke couldn't have known is that even though he had been in the land of the dead for just one night, three hundred years had passed in the land of the living. His daughter, and all that he had known, had died long ago.

Despite Morphia's pleading Yorke wouldn't keep his promise to her until he had found his daughter again, and when he discovered the awful truth he took the flower that he had lost so much to have and threw himself into the sea in this grief, leaving

Morphia alone. Lost in the bright world of the living, she tried to make her way back home, but couldn't find her way to the crack at the centre of the earth. She wandered helpless, with no one to guide her. Unused as she was to light and to life she became confused, and ever more helpless.

She had only been absent from the Kingdom of Death for three days when her father learned what had happened and came himself to the land of the living to find her. He crossed oceans and continents, climbed mountains and crossed valleys, leaving no stone unturned in his desperate search for his daughter. After many days' searching he found her sitting, as helpless as a babe, on a rock, far from anywhere.

'My child,' he said, crying in his relief, 'there you are! How happy I am to see you again, and how worried I have been that you were gone. Come, let us leave this accursed place and go back home, where we will be safe from this light and noise.'

But his daughter lifted her head and looked at him blankly, not knowing what he was saying. And with horror he saw no recognition in her eyes, for although she had been away from the land of the dead for just three days, she had spent nearly a thousand

142

years in the Kingdom of the Living, and had quite forgotten who she had ever been.

In great sorrow Death left her there, and he vowed a terrible vengeance on this world that had done such a thing to his child. He cursed the fear that men have of death that had caused the loss of his daughter, and he determined that from that moment on, as payment for what they had done to him, men would be harbingers of death far greater than he, bringing about what they hated most. And so war and greed and cruelty entered mens' hearts and multiplied, causing man's biggest enemy from that moment on to be himself.

And Morphia still wanders the earth, lifeless and deathless, knowing nothing of who she is or what she should do. Wherever she goes men are filled with fear and uncertainly, and their eyes are blinded to the truth, leading them astray and into peril. For this reason her father renamed her, and so it is that because of one man's trespass into the land of the dead, Confusion was introduced into the world.

A True Reflection

The hero of this story is the great Uglow, and he came from a long line of mirror makers. His father before him had been a mirror maker, and his father before him. Uglow's mother had also been a great mirror maker, as had his grandmother before that. Everyone in Uglow's family had made mirrors for kings and queens and nobles and many other important people, and Uglow was no exception. People would come from far and wide to him for a mirror, and the ones he made were more beautiful than anyone had ever seen before.

That Uglow was a master craftsman was not in doubt, but over the years he had become bored with producing such fine mirrors. He would watch listlessly as all the fine gentlemen and ladies came in and out of his shop, barking orders at their servants and hiding behind fake smiles to each other. He began to wince as they admired themselves in his creations, and found that he had no love for his art anymore. He longed to do more than just reflect the world's appearance back at itself; he wanted to show the world as it truly was instead. A mirror was all very well, but it wouldn't tell you anything that anyone else with eyes could. One day, as he sat deep in despair in his shop, he suddenly had an idea.

'I've got it!' he said to his apprentice. 'Shut up the shop, for today I start work on a new masterpiece!'

And so Uglow closed his shop for the day to much grumbling from the fine nobles in their even finer clothes, and he started work on something that no mirror maker had ever tried before. He stayed locked up in his workshop for weeks, barely eating or sleeping, working away furiously.

'What is it he's doing?' people wondered. 'Whatever can Uglow be working on?'

The nobles, concerned that they hadn't seen him for some weeks now and that they had nowhere to buy their fine mirrors from, came to his workshop to ask him what he was doing.

'I'm working on my finest creation yet,' he told them proudly. 'It's something that'll change the world forever. I'm making a mirror that will show people not as they appear on the outside, but as they actually are. Can you imagine such a thing? How much better the world would be!'

But the nobles just laughed at him.

'Uglow,' they said, wiping tears from their eyes, 'what you say is impossible! Come now, stick to what you're good at, and leave off this nonsense. It cannot be done, and even if it could, who would want something like that?'

But Uglow wouldn't listen to them. His shop remained closed as the weeks turned into months and the months turned into years, and still he toiled away.

His friends became worried about him, and came to his workshop.

'Uglow,' they said, 'you must stop this at once. What you're trying to do is dangerous, for no one would like to see themself as they really are. We beg of you, please stop this madness.'

But Uglow wouldn't stop. He was convinced that his mirror of truth would be more important than people's opinions. Such a thing would not only make him the most famous mirror maker history had ever known, but by reflecting men's hearts back at them he was convinced that he would change the world for the better.

'If people could see themselves as they really are,' he said to himself, 'they would think twice about being unkind to each other. How much better the world would be!'

Finally, after three years, he announced to the world that he had completed his masterpiece. A huge crowd gathered around Uglow's shop while he sent his apprentice to fetch the already famous mirror of truth. When the mirror had been brought to him, wrapped in a cloth, Uglow set it down in front of the crowd and stood behind it.

'Who would like to be the first person to see their true reflection?' he asked.

A beautifully dressed, rich young lady nervously stepped up to stand in front of the mirror. The crowd cheered the brave volunteer. Uglow smiled warmly and waited for her to prepare herself.

'Are you ready?' Uglow asked after a few minutes.

The nervous young lady nodded. The crowd held its breath. With a flourish, Uglow whipped away the cloth and the woman saw her reflection. She gasped. The crowd gasped. Uglow watched the woman intently. She took a step towards her reflection, peering at it searchingly. Finally she stepped back.

'I look beautiful!" she announced, smiling. 'Look how beautiful I really am!'

The crowd cheered. One by one they stepped up to examine themselves in the mirror of truth, and one by one they went away overjoyed with how lovely their true selves were. It was a miracle! How much did Uglow want for such a mirror, they asked, they would pay anything. But Uglow wouldn't sell. How could he sell his life's masterpiece, his gift to the world?

All day the rich and the famous of the town stepped up to Uglow's mirror to admire themselves as they really were, and each and every one of them was delighted with how beautiful they looked. Uglow was promised fame and fortune beyond his wildest dreams by his grateful customers, and he couldn't have been happier. As it grew dark the overjoyed craftsman stepped out from behind his mirror and wrapped it up again to take back to his workshop.

Uglow whistled to himself as he carried the shrouded mirror home. He was the talk of the town! If he thought he had been famous before, that was nothing to how he was now. He was loved by all, and the warm glow of popularity spread through him deliciously. He'd been right all along; people did want to see themselves as they really were.

It was only as he put the mirror away carefully in a corner of his workshop that it occurred to him that it was a bit odd that *everyone* had been happy with what they had seen. When he had been making the mirror the version that he had seen of himself had been, not ugly exactly, but certainly startling. What had it looked like again? Uglow lifted a corner of the covering of the mirror to have a look once more, but gasped in horror at what he saw.

The mirror reflected back at him just his reflection, nothing more. He peered closer. There was nothing in the least bit special about what he saw at all. In shock, Uglow turned around and saw a very similar looking mirror in the other corner of the room. This one reflected back at him a grasping, ugly man, one whose head had been turned by promises of fame and fortune and who had abandoned his dreams for money. The reflection grinned at him and rubbed its hands in glee.

Uglow stood still in shock. His apprentice had brought the wrong mirror! All anyone had seen had been their normal reflection after all. He knew that when they saw themselves as they truly were his rich and powerful customers would be furious. He would never sell a mirror again.

In great sadness, Uglow realised that there was only one thing to be done. He couldn't ignore what he had made and the good it could do the world. Quickly, he looked around to make sure that no one was looking, and then he kicked his great creation for all he was worth, smashing it into a thousand pieces.

The very next day, Uglow took his mirror of truth to the king, who was delighted with what he saw. He gave Uglow his daughter's hand in marriage in recognition of such a miraculous achievement, and Uglow became the richest and most famous mirror maker the world has ever known. His great mirror still hangs in the royal palace, and all who look into it are delighted to see reflected back at them exactly what they would hope to see.

The Mountain of Gold

Far away and just as long ago a whisper of a rumour came to the court of a great king. The rumour spoke of a mountain full of gold in a distant land. It was unmistakeable, so the rumour said, for it was the biggest of any mountain around it, and had a single solitary tree at its summit. But the gold in this mountain couldn't be mined, for this mountain wasn't made of rock, but of iron.

The king was a greedy, avaricious man. He had vast chambers full of treasure, and nothing gave him more pleasure than to count his money and gaze upon his riches. This kind of talk of mountains of gold excited him, and he hungrily sent men forth to find the mountain and see if the rumour was true. The men travelled for many days and many nights, and finally they came to a land they had never been to before. In this land they found a range of mountains, but there was one mountain that towered above its neighbours, and this peak, they were delighted to see, had a singly solitary tree at its summit. When they came to the mountain they discovered that it was indeed not made from rock, but from iron.

But they also found something that the rumour hadn't mentioned. Next to the single tree at the summit of the mountain stood a well, full and evidently in use. The men found this puzzling, for they were in a desolate, inhospitable place, and couldn't see any signs of anyone living for a great many miles around. As tired and thirsty as they were, they didn't drink from the well, for they feared that the waters from such a place might be enchanted.

They roamed the summit and slopes of the mountain for many hours, but they found neither a way into the mountain nor any sign of any living inhabitant. They had given up any hope of finding either, and had started to turn their minds to what to tell their king when the youngest of the group, weary from his day's labours on the steep slopes, lost his footing and fell headlong into a deep gorge in the mountainside. In horror, his companions rushed to him, but he had fallen down a fissure in the iron too deep and with sides to steep for any of them to climb down after him, and they had no rope between them. So far had the boy fallen they could barely see him. In desperation the called down to him, but he lay unconscious, and barely breathing. The men were distraught, but night was coming on fast, and unable to rescue their friend they were forced by the cold and the dark to leave the treacherous slopes to make camp at the foot of the mountain.

They awoke early the next morning, sick with worry and terrified that their friend wouldn't have survived the night out in the open. They jumped up, and were just about to go out to the mountain to try to rescue him when they were amazed to see him lying in their midst, peaceably asleep. What's more, someone had obviously tended to him, for a bandage had been tied around his head to staunch a deep wound there, and his right leg had been tied to a splint to set it straight. Fearing enchantment again they stood in silence around him, unsure of what to do, but at that moment he woke quite naturally, and opened his eyes to see his companions surrounding him. Immediately they pressed in on him, all clamouring to know how he had got out of the gorge, and who had mended his wounds.

He told them that he had been lying more dead than alive at the bottom of the gorge when out of a tiny hole in the iron had emerged a dwarf. He took fright at seeing the boy lying there, and was just about to run back into his hole when the boy called to him in a feeble whisper.

'Please,' he said, 'please help me. I have fallen from the top of this gorge and I fear my leg is broken. My companions can't get down to me and have been forced to retreat by the darkness. I am so cold and feeling faint. Please help me, I fear I will die if I am left the night here on my own.'

On hearing this the dwarf paused for a second, and then scurried back into his hole. The boy closed his eyes in despair, but when he opened them again he saw standing in front of him a whole crowd of dwarves.

'Please don't be afraid,' said the first dwarf that had come across him, 'we don't mean to hurt you.'

The dwarves immediately set about tending to the amazed boy's wounded head and leg. As they worked he asked them,

'But where did you come from? Do you live in the mountain?'

'We do indeed,' came the reply.

'And tell me,' the boy asked feverishly, 'is it true what people say, is this mountain really full of gold?'

'Why, yes it is,' the dwarf said. 'We are the guardians of the gold. We delight in it and grow as much as we can every day. We need it as you people need food or water. If we were ever to be separated from it it would cause us great pain, we don't need it for trinkets or your funny coins as your kind do, but we love it and need it for its own sake.'

By now the dwarves had finished bandaging the boy's head and legs, and they wrapped him in warm blankets and approached him gravely with food and water.

'Please, eat and drink,' the lead dwarf told him. 'When you've regained enough of your strength we'll take you back to your companions - down here is no place for one such as you to spend the night.'

The boy ate and drank obediently. The food was magnificent, like nothing he had ever tasted before. Immediately a great warmth and strength coursed through him. The drink they gave him too was like nothing he had ever known. Like the food it was warm and nourishing, and the boy felt that if he never had anything else to eat and drink in his whole life he wouldn't mind one bit.

'Why are you helping me like this?' he asked the dwarf, perplexed.

The dwarf looked back at him in confusion.

'But you are in pain, and need help,' he said. 'You would surely die without us, why would we not help you?'

And with that the dwarves picked the boy up and climbed up the sheer face of the gorge with him on their backs. How such little people managed to carry him up a flat wall many tens of times taller than either of them the boy couldn't say, but he hadn't been scared once. The dwarves had him at the top of the gorge in no time, and were as good as their word, carrying him down the mountain to where his companions slept and laying him gently down, whereupon he fell into a deep and peaceful sleep.

'And the next thing I knew,' the boy said, 'was you all standing around me as I woke up. I tell you, it was the dwarves, they saved my life.'

Full of gratitude, the men searched up and down the mountain for the dwarves to thank them for their great kindness, but they couldn't find a single one. As they looked closely at the surface of the mountain though they started to notice many holes in the iron, far too small for them to fit through, but that could easily admit a dwarf. As a show of thanks they left a small bag of all the gold they had outside one of these entrances, and started the long journey back to their king.

Many days later they returned to the palace. The king, eager to here if rumours of the mountain of gold were true, demanded to see them immediately. When they told him that they had indeed found the mountain, and it was full to the brim with gold, he was overjoyed.

'But how can we get to it?' he asked greedily. 'You say the mountain is made of iron?'

'There is no way that I can see, sire' said one of the men. 'And it would appear that the gold already has owners.'

And the men recounted the tale of how the boy's fall down the gorge and how the dwarves had saved his life.

'These dwarves are kind and peaceful,' the boy said. 'They saved my life and asked for nothing in return. We should leave them be. Besides, there's no way into the mountain, for all of the dwarves' entrances are far too small for a man to fit through.'

At this the king flew into a rage.

'We shall see whose gold it is!' he cried. 'We will see what these dwarves have to say when I'm knocking at their door with a sword in my hand!'

And, despite the protests of the men, he gave orders for a huge army to be assembled, and the next day sallied forth with it to the mountain of gold. On reaching the mountain he and his army ranged its slopes, desperately trying to find any way in, but they couldn't. Day after day they searched, and day after day they were unable to find a way to reach the mountain's core of riches.

But on the seventh day the king was suddenly struck with an idea. He pulled the army back to some distance away, out of sight of the mountain, and then, remembering his men's story, he set out alone for the peak, dressed simply in rags. There he waited until nightfall, whereupon he lay down on the slopes of the mountain and moaned piteously.

He hadn't been lying like this for very long when the king was rewarded by the approach of a concerned looking dwarf who had appeared from a hole in the iron so small the king hadn't even seen it. The dwarf approached the king anxiously.

'What is the trouble, tall man?' he asked. These mountain slopes are no place for one such as yourself at night. Are you injured at all?'

'Yes, yes I am!' the king lied. 'I have fallen and now find that I can't move. And this night is so bitterly cold, I feel that I will die if I am left here in the open like this. Is there any shelter hereabouts? Perhaps you could take me to your home, did I see you come from inside this mountain?'

'You did indeed,' said the dwarf, 'and it's certainly warm in there. I wish with all my heart I could take you into my home, but the entrance is far too small for one such as yourself. Don't you have any companions nearby with a fire or shelter I could perhaps take you to?'

'Alas,' the king lied again, 'I am all alone. I come from a kingdom many days' travel from here, where I was exiled by the cruel and wicked king who rules there. I have travelled by myself every since, searching for somewhere I might call home. Oh! But are you sure I can't come into the mountain?'

'Why, you poor man!' the dwarf exclaimed. 'I'm afraid to say that it would take a great many of us to dig you a tunnel big enough to admit you, by which time I fear that you'll have frozen to death. But take cheer, I'll return momentarily with thick blankets and pillows for you, and hot soup and bread to warm your belly. My kinsmen and I will heal whatever injuries you might have, and see that you come to no harm.'

And so saying the dwarf made to return to where he had come from when the king jumped up and threw him into a bag before he knew what was happening.

Crowing with delight, the king brought the struggling dwarf back to the army, where he gave orders for the little man to be tied up and brought before him. The soldiers reluctantly did as they were told, and the bound dwarf was carried into the presence of the king, who was now clothed once more in his robes and crown.

'So,' the gloating king said to his poor captive, 'you see I am not quite so helpless after all. But I'm not here to show you how much stronger I am than you. I am mean to take from you all the gold that you're hoarding in that mountain of yours. Tell me how to do that, and I'll spare your life.'

But the dwarf didn't give the king the answer he wanted.

'Your majesty,' the dwarf said, 'I'm afraid I can't do as you ask. My countrymen and I are guardians of the gold you speak of, and we won't deliver it into a tyrant's hands. We delight in the gold and care for it, and we would die a long and painful death without it. I beg of you, leave the gold where it is, for that's where it should be, not around a rich man's neck or in a greedy merchant's pocket. It has more value for its own sake. Please, leave it be.'

This answer enraged the king. He tortured the dwarf, demanding that the dwarf and his kind dig tunnels to grant his army access to the mountain, but his prisoner refused. The king was certain there must be a way for him to get to the gold, and he continued to torture the exhausted dwarf. Finally, his captive could bear it no longer.

'Very well,' gasped the dwarf, by now on the brink of death, 'there is a way you might enter the mountain.'

At this the king jumped up and motioned to the torturers to stop their grisly work.

'Drink from our well,' the dwarf told him. 'If you do this you will find yourself small enough to get what you desire.'

The king leaned closer.

'Inside the mountain, will I find gold?'

The dwarf raised his head one last time.

'You'll find all the gold you could ever want,' he replied sadly, before dying in the king's arms.

The king lost no time. He called for his blacksmiths and cloth weavers and told them to make clothes and weapons, pick axes, spades and carts, for an army of dwarf sized men. For five days and nights the camp was full of the din of the clash of iron on steel as swords, shields, axes and armour were made, while the cloth makers worked tirelessly to produce clothes for the king's demand. Once everything was done to his satisfaction he assembled his army and marched them to the top of the mountain, where the dwarves' well lay. He ordered a bucket to be drawn from it, and fell upon the cool, clear water, greedily gulping down huge, desperate mouthfuls. Once he had drunk his fill he ordered every single one of his soldiers to do the same. Once they had all drunk as much as they could they stood and waited, no one but the king quite sure of what to expect.

It was the king who felt it first. He started to feel that the world around him was bigger. He looked up and saw that the well seemed to be growing taller, as did his men. He reached out to his captain, who was stood right next to him, but he found that he couldn't reach him any more. In confusion he looked at his arm. It seemed to be shorter. He suddenly realised that it was not that everything else was growing, but that he was shrinking. He looked back at his army and saw to his delight that his men were shrinking too. Shouting for joy, he immediately called for more water to be drawn from the well and ordered his men to drink again. They drank until the well ran dry, and when they had done so the king found to his delight that he and his army were no bigger than the dwarves themselves. With a cry of excitement, the king ordered the men to put on their small clothing and armour and pick up their dwarf sized swords and spades and follow him into the mountain.

The men poured into the dwarves' mountain home and found themselves in a bewildering network of tunnels that zig zagged and criss crossed each other for miles inside the iron. Unused as they were to being underground the men soon became lost and fearful, but the king urged them on, driving them forward towards what he felt sure was the heart of the mountain. The dwarves, terrified and knowing nothing of swords and shields were chased away. They fled from the mountain, never to return.

The army rampaged through the barren tunnels for some time, and were starting to doubt that any gold lay within the mountain when they suddenly came upon a huge cavern filled with huge piles of gold, more gold than any of them had ever seen in their lives. With cries of excitement they greedily feel upon the precious metal, carving great holes out of the mounds and loading their carts with as much as they could hold. They quarried all that day and the next, they quarried until their hands were raw, yet they still had not taken half the gold.

Slowly, the men began to notice that they were having to stoop to fit through the tunnels as they mined, where once they could walk through without ducking at all. In alarm, they realised that the properties of the dwarves' well water were wearing off, and hurriedly called for more to be brought to them, but the well now stood empty.

'Let us go,' they said to each other. 'We've taken quite enough, and if we don't leave now we'll be trapped in this mountain.'

One by one they started to leave to the safety of outside, squeezing their rapidly growing limbs out of the rock tunnels as fast as they could. But there was one man who was too distracted to notice the change that was taking place as he dug hungrily.

'Where are you going?' the greedy king shouted after his men as one by one the left him. 'We have much more yet to quarry!'

But even as he shouted he was starting to return to his former size.

'Don't be a fool!' his men shouted back. 'Come out now, or you'll never be able to leave!'

But the king didn't listen. He couldn't take his eyes from all the gold around him, and continued to dig for all he was worth. Too late did he turn around to leave through the small tunnel that would take him back to the outside, only to find that he was now too big to fit through it. In horror he looked down at his arms and legs and saw them growing before his very eyes. Desperate now, he flung himself at the tiny tunnel's entrance, trying in vain to contort himself into every shape that he could think of to escape, but it was no use. He was trapped. Surrounded, as the dwarf had said, by all the gold he could ever want.

The men, finding that their king had become entombed in the mountain, fled. With the gold they now had none of them had any need to go back to soldiering, and they scattered, each of them departing with his gold to make a better life for himself.

The dwarves too had fled far from the mountain, and wandered through hill and vale, over seas and across deserts until they eventually settled once more and founded a new city of their own. By this time many years had passed, and they too, now far away from their well, had started to grow. By the time they founded their town there was nothing in height to separate them from ordinary men, and indeed, after a few generations they forgot to call themselves dwarves at all.

Their town became prosperous, but as the dwarves' height had gown so had their greed, and so it was with great interest that, many years later, their king listened to whisper of a rumour of a faraway mountain with a single tree at its summit that was full of gold. The gold, it was said, was guarded by a king who lived within the mountain and guarded it jealously. But guardian or no guardian, talk of this much gold excited the townsfolk greatly, and led by their king they set forth for the mountain, intent on stealing the gold for themselves, and grimly resolved to kill anyone who stood in their way.

The Magic Lamp

Billy Christie lived in a big house at the end of a long road in a small town called Combray. He lived with his mother and father and sister and brother who all loved him very much. He did well at school and was good at sports, but none of this mattered very much to Billy. Because Billy had no friends.

Billy's family had always travelled. His father had a job that meant they moved every year or two, and Billy was always starting a new school, and that meant having to get to know a whole new group of people again who already had their own friends. He'd joined his current school halfway through the year, which had only made things harder. Billy wasn't particularly good at making new friends, but at this new school especially no one seemed to like him. No one would sit next to him in class or at lunch, no one would talk to him in the playground either or let him join in their games, and he knew that they all talked about him and laughed at him behind his back. And as if this wasn't bad enough, the biggest bully in the school had taken a special dislike to him.

That boy's name was Martin Proud. Martin picked on Billy all the time, and this meant that everyone else was as nasty to him as they could be as well. Martin made sure that Billy's days at school were spent running from class to class, trying to avoid anyone's attention and keeping to himself as much as he could, for whenever Martin had a chance he would tease him or punch him or hurt him in some way, and everyone else would just laugh.

The journeys to and from school were the worse, with the long waits on the train platform. There was nowhere to hide on the train platform, and nothing to stop Martin and his friends getting on the same carriage when then saw you, either. The train rides were a long twenty minutes each, and most people at the school got on and off at the same stop as Billy, meaning that he was guaranteed forty minutes of torment a day, even if he managed to avoid everyone all day at school.

Billy was miserable. His parents, like all grown ups, didn't understand, and his brother and sister were too busy worrying about their own lives to care about his. Besides, they were much older, and didn't even go to the same school as him. He would dread the start of each new school day, lying in bed in the mornings before his alarm went off with a sick feeling in his stomach, praying for a fire at the school, or an unseasonable blizzard, or even that he might find himself really ill, anything that would mean he didn't have to go to school. But nothing like that ever happened. Each day surely enough followed the next, and Billy grew steadily more and more unhappy. That is, until he found the lamp.

He was at home playing in the garden when he found it. He'd been digging trenches in the flowerbeds for his toy soldiers, something he knew he shouldn't really be doing, when his fingers touched something hard and metallic in the ground under one of the big rosebushes. Puzzled, he scraped away the soft earth and saw a golden glint peeping back at him. Thinking that he'd found some real buried treasure, he excitedly unearthed whatever it was and held it up to the light.

It certainly wasn't treasure, or at least not the kind of treasure that Billy had ever seen before. It was an old fashioned oil lamp, the sort of thing he'd seen in story books. It was made of bronze, not gold, but it was clearly very, very old. It was so covered in soil that Billy could barely see any of it at all, and he set about scraping away the mud and rubbing off the dirt to get a better look at it. He hadn't been rubbing it for very long, and had managed to get most of the mud from it, when Billy suddenly felt a jolt in his hand. He sat up. He could have sworn that the jolt had come from the lamp. What's more, it had felt like it had come from *inside* it. Cautiously, Billy rubbed the lamp again, and this time dropped it in shock as he definitely, without a doubt this time, felt something stirring within.

He jumped to his feet and stood for some minutes, staring at the lamp. It looked harmless enough. Ugly even. But what Billy had felt in his hand scared him, and he looked down at the little thing with mistrust. If he had left the lamp alone at that moment, as he had half a mind to do, his life would have been very different, but as with all little boys, eventually curiosity got the better of him and he picked the lamp up once more.

He examined it closely. It was quite plain really, with a few lines in the metal running down it here and there to serve as decoration, but it was actually very boring. He shook it. Nothing in it rattled. He tried to take the lid off but that was stuck down fast. No matter how much Billy pulled it wouldn't budge one inch. Forgetting his fear, he rubbed the lamp again.

If Billy had dropped the lamp before, he fairly threw it away this time. It had given such an explosive jolt that Billy had felt that he was going to be blown to bits, and he knew that he had to get it as far away from him as possible. He hurled it as far as he could as if it were a grenade and fell to the floor, screwing his eyes tight, waiting for whatever bad thing that was surely going to happen to happen.

But nothing did happen. Billy opened his eyes cautiously and found that his garden was just as he had left it a few seconds ago. His toy soldiers were still there. There was a blackbird still singing in an apple tree by his house, and most important of all, Billy appeared to still have all of his arms and his legs and not a scratch on him.

Relieved, and feeling a little silly, Billy stood up again. But he had been wrong. His garden was not quite as it had been before he had rubbed the lamp. For now, at his feet, stood a tiny little man wearing a long blue coat covered in golden stars looking at him with an annoyed look on his face.

'Hullo,' said Billy.

And then asked, quite sensibly,

'Where did you come from?'

'I came from the lamp,' said the little man. 'Why did you throw me all the way over there?'

'I'm sorry,' said Billy, 'I thought you were going to explode.'

'Oh,' said the little man.

This answer seemed to satisfy him, and he stopped looking quite so aggrieved.

'I beg your pardon,' said Billy, 'but what do you mean you came from the lamp?'

'That's where I live,' said the little man.

Now it was Billy's turn to have nothing to say.

'You summoned me by rubbing on the lamp, now I have to grant you a wish.'

'Oh,' said Billy politely, 'you don't need to worry about anything like that. I didn't mean to disturb you.'

The little man was dumbfounded.

'You mean to tell me,' he said incredulously, 'that you don't want anything at all, that you have no wish in all the world?'

Billy stood for a moment, looking about the empty garden.

'I do sometimes wish,' he said sadly, 'that I had someone to play with my soldiers with me.'

At this the little man gave a twinkly little smile and snapped his fingers.

'Then I shall play with you, young man. Are these your soldiers here? Gosh, they're nearly as big as me…'

And that was how Billy found the lamp, and met the best friend he had ever had.

It was one of the happiest afternoons of Billy's life. He had never had anyone to play with before, and the little man was a wonderful playmate. He would run and jump and hide and play act and brought the soldiers to life in ways that never happened when Billy played on his own. The little man was funny too, and made Billy laugh until he cried, rolling over onto his back and kicking his legs into the air for sheer joy. Billy was having so much fun that he quite forgot what time it was, and it was nearly dark when his mother called him in for dinner.

His mother's call had no sooner ended then the little man said a quick goodbye, ran off down the garden and jumped back into the lamp. Disappointed that his new friend wasn't going to join him for dinner, Billy set about gathering up all of his soldiers, and as he did so he noticed in the fading light that one of the little man's golden stars had fallen off his coat. Thinking that he would like to give it back to his new friend, he carefully put the star in his pocket. Then he went to the bottom of the garden, picked up the funny little lamp, and went inside for his dinner.

That night, as soon as he was alone in bed, Billy took the lamp out and rubbed it again. This time he kept hold of it tightly with both hands. It gave a violent shudder, and suddenly the little man appeared sitting on Billy's covers and looking at him curiously.

'You have another wish already?' the little man asked.

'No,' said Billy, 'I just wondered what your name was.'

The man looked confused.

'No one's ever asked me my name before,' he admitted.

'Mine's Billy,' said Billy, what's yours?'

'I'm Marcel,' said the little man, thrusting out a tiny hand, which Billy took between the end of his finger and thumb and shook very solemnly, 'it's a pleasure to meet you.'

'Can we play again tomorrow?' Billy asked eagerly. 'I mean, only if you'd like to, that is.'

'We certainly can,' declared Marcel, 'your wish is my command!'

And with that he jumped back into the lamp as quickly as he had appeared.

Billy carefully put the lamp down on the floor next to his bed. He was just about the turn out the light when he noticed that another of the little man's stars had fallen off his coat. Very carefully, he picked it up and put it with the other one that he had collected in the garden in a small wooden box on his bookshelf.

He took the lamp with him to school the next day. He took great care that no one should see it, for he felt sure that if it was discovered people would only tease him about it. Through the taunts and laughter of Martin Proud and his friends he took comfort in knowing that the lamp was with him, and its reassuring glint every time he opened his bag helped him through the day.

Marcel was as good as his word. As soon as Billy had got home from school and laid out his toy soldiers in the garden then the little man appeared. They played all afternoon again, and this time it was Marcel who was laughing so hard that he didn't hear Billy's mother calling to announce dinner as the sun set. When he noticed

Billy gathering up his soldiers he made to jump back into the lamp, but he was brought up short by Billy saying shyly,

'You don't have to go back in there you know, you could stay for dinner if you'd like.'

'Oh but I'm afraid I can't,' said Marcel, 'I must go back into my lamp as soon as the wish is completed.'

But just as he was about to jump back into his lamp he stopped again and turned to the little boy.

'No one has ever asked me to dinner before,' he said. 'Thank you.'

And with that he vanished once more, leaving another gold star from his coat behind which Billy carefully picked up and put in his pocket.

That night Billy rubbed the lamp and summoned Marcel once again.

'Another wish?' asked Marcel. 'What would you like this time?'

'Oh, nothing,' said Billy, 'what would you like to do?'

Marcel froze.

'Why would you ask me what I want to do?' he asked.

'I don't know,' said Billy, 'I mean, if we're friends, we don't always have to play my games, we can play your games too if you'd like. We are friends, aren't we?' he asked hopefully.

At this Marcel seemed quite taken aback.

'I've never had a friend before,' he told Billy.

'Nor have I,' Billy admitted, 'would you like to be mine?'

The little man looked up at Billy very shyly.

'Yes, yes I would,' he said. 'Yes please.'

And the two talked long into the night. Billy told Marcel all about his life, how he had often moved around from school to school and had never had a chance to make any friends because he had never lived anywhere for very long. He told him about his mum and his dad and his sister and his brother, about how they were all nice enough, but they didn't really understand him, and were too preoccupied with grown up things to care about him properly. And he told Marcel about the bullying. About how every day he dreaded school more than the last. About the cruel taunts and how Martin, the biggest boy in the school, would hit him whenever he could, but it was the teasing and laughing that hurt the most. He told him how nowhere was safe, not even the journey into school on the train, and how helpless he felt, and no one understood.

And Marcel told Billy all about his long, lonely life in the lamp. He had lived in it for many thousands of years, and he was far older than Billy. It was comfortable enough in there, he said, but it was just him, and there was no one to talk to, let alone play with.

'But in all those thousands of years,' Billy said, 'I can't be the first person who has rubbed on the lamp. That's why you come out, isn't it? When someone rubs on the lamp?'

'It is,' said Marcel. 'And you're right, lots of other people have rubbed on the lamp before you and called me, but all they ever want is for me to grant them wishes. No one has even asked me my name in all these years except for you.'

And that was when Billy noticed that another star had fallen off Marcel's coat.

'I don't know who made your coat,' he said, 'but they really were very clumsy. Every time I see you one of the stars falls off it, at this rate you'll have none left on there at all!'

At this Marcel went quite pale.

'Oh, don't worry,' Billy said, 'I'm sure I can sew them back on, even though your coat is so small. I've kept them all for you here, look.'

And he showed Marcel the box where he had been keeping the stars that had fallen from the little man's coat. Marcel took the stars very gravely and looked at them sadly as they lay in his hand.

'I'm afraid that these can never be sewn back on. I may have lived for much longer than you, but I can't live forever. Every time I leave my lamp I lose another star from my coat. When all the stars are gone, that will be the end of me.'

'Why don't you just stay out of your lamp then?' Billy asked. 'If you don't go back in, you can't lose a star coming back out can you?'

'It doesn't work like that.' Marcel told him. 'I can't stay out for as long as I want. If I stay out for too long I'm pulled back in, whether I like it or not.'

'Well that's fine!' said Billy cheerily. 'Look how many stars you still have left!'

But then seeing the look on the little man's face he said added, 'Don't worry, I'll never use up all of your stars.'

The two played together in the garden again the next day, and the next, and the next. Billy would often call Marcel from the lamp in the evenings as well, and they would read together in bed or tell each other stories well into the night. The days that once seemed to last an eternity for Billy, full of teasing and bullying, would now fly by. He would take the lamp with him to school every day, and sit and wait impatiently, barely hearing a word that his teachers or anyone else said to him, desperate for the moment when the bell would go and he could rush home and play with his new friend.

The days turned into weeks and the weeks turned into months and those months turned into summer and Billy had never been happier. His parents decided that they liked Combray, and told Billy that they were going to stay where they were. A couple of the other children at school had even started to talk to him nicely on the final few days of term. The summer holidays began, and suddenly Billy's sleepy town was awash with children whooping and hollering and laughing, chasing each other through the streets, playing down by the woods and swimming in the river. Billy could hear the shouts of games and his schoolmates having all kinds of fun on the village green from his garden, but no one ever invited him to play.

Not that he minded one bit. He and Marcel were busy making their own fun. They would play in his garden all day long, from the break of day until last thing at night, when Billy's mother would call him in for his dinner, and Billy would reluctantly collect up all of his soldiers while Marcel returned to his lamp. Sometimes, if they were sure they wouldn't bump into any of the other local children, they would go down to the woods and play there, climbing trees and building forts and damming rivers. The days were long and the evenings warm, and the two playmates wanted for nothing from anyone.

They played together so long and so often that they both quite lost track of how many times Billy had called for Marcel, and it was with horror that Billy looked down at Marcel one day as they sat playing by the rose bush where they had first met, and realised that there was just one star left on the little man's coat. In desperation Marcel took his coat off and they examined it thoroughly, inside and out, but as hard as they looked it was clear that just a single gold star remained on the Marcel's magnificent blue coat. Billy's eyes brimmed with tears.

'Don't cry,' the little man said with a weak smile. 'I still have one star left; we can play together one more time. Your wish is my command.'

But Billy meant to keep his promise. He knew that this would be the last time he would see his friend.

That evening, when Billy's mother called him in for his dinner he could hardly bear to gather in his soldiers. Marcel came and sat on his shoulder as he did so, unwilling to jump back into his lamp. Finally, as darkness fell and they heard Billy's mother calling him in for a third time Billy knew that he could put things off no longer.

'Good bye,' he said to Marcel, as the little man hopped into the palm of his hand. 'I shall never forget you. I'm sorry I used up all your stars,' he added, gulping.

'There's no need to cry,' Marcel told him. 'I'd never known what it was to have a friend or to play until this summer. It's been the happiest time I've ever known, and I would rather use up every star on my coat playing with you than keep them all and carry on as I was. They weren't worth anything until I met you, but I wouldn't take back a single one that I've lost this summer. You will always be my friend, and I'll never forget you either.'

And suddenly for the first time Billy saw just how old the little man was, and how lonely. Marcel looked right into Billy's eyes and delivered a solemn little bow. Billy blinked, and when he opened his eyes again the little man had disappeared back into his lamp once more. Billy sat quite still in the fading light for a long time, looking at down at where his friend had been. Then, as his mother called his name for the fourth time, he picked up the tiny golden star that Marcel had left behind and went in for his dinner.

Billy didn't play again in the garden for the rest of the summer. In fact, he barely left his room. He would sit on his bed and with the lamp and the little wooden box where he had collected all of Marcel's stars and look at them, remembering the little man. Every day he was tempted to rub the lamp, to call his friend one last time to come and play with him, but he knew that he couldn't. He kept his promise.

School stared again, and it was clear that the summer holidays hadn't changed what anyone thought about Billy. Martin Proud certainly hadn't forgotten about him, and the teasing and taunting and bullying continued just as it had. Billy still took the lamp with him to school every day, as even if he could never see him again it cheered him to think that his friend was with him still.

Billy's first two weeks back at school passed by with nothing that you'd call out of the ordinary. He was kicked and punched when the teacher's back was turned, tripped up in the corridors and teased horribly in the playground, but none of this was new for Billy. The only person with any kind words for him at all was a new boy who had started after the holidays. His name was Simon, and unlike everyone else he was kind to Billy. He picked Billy up when Martin had just tripped him, he smiled in sympathy, not enjoyment, whenever Billy was humiliated by Martin's teasing. He didn't point and laugh like everyone else. As Simon was new he didn't have any friends either, and the two of them took solace in each other, hiding from Martin and his friends at lunchtimes.

It was in Billy's third week back at school that it happened. He was standing on the busy train platform with Simon, waiting for the 8.25 that would take them to school when he saw Martin Proud, head and shoulders above everyone else, pushing his was towards him. An involuntary sound of fear escaped his lips.

'Don't worry,' Simon whispered. 'He probably won't event speak to us.'

But Martin did speak to them.

'Hello Billy no mates,' he said with a wicked grin. 'We haven't spoken in a couple of days, have we?'

Keeping his eyes fixed on the floor, Billy didn't answer.

'What do you have for lunch today?' Martin asked. 'I've forgotten mine.'

'He doesn't have anything for you!' Simon said.

Martin ignored him and spun Billy round, grabbing his backpack. There was a crowd around them now, jeering and laughing at Billy.

'Get off!' Billy cried, trying to pull his bag back from Martin.

But Martin was far too big and strong. He wrenched open Billy's backpack, breaking the zipper, and reached inside greedily.

'I don't have anything!' Billy cried in vain, still struggling.

Martin's expression turned to one of confusion as his fingers closed around something quite unexpected.

'What's this?' he cried, pulling Billy's lamp from his bag. 'What are you doing with a silly old pot?'

Everyone began to laugh as Martin held the lamp aloft.

'Look at Billy's stupid little pot!' he shouted. 'What do you have this for?'

'Give that back!' cried Billy.

A smile lit up Martin's face.

'I think I'll keep it,' he said.

Billy was aghast. Forgetting his bag, he reached out with both hands and snatched the lamp back from Martin, surprising them both with his strength.

'No!' Billy shouted, hugging the lamp close to him. 'This is mine, take anything else you want!'

But Martin didn't like not getting his own way, and he especially didn't like being told no by Billy, of all people, in front of everyone like this. He grabbed the lamp, but Billy wouldn't let go.

'But I want this,' he said grimly. 'You'll give it to me won't you?'

And he tried to snatch it away, but Billy held on doggedly. Soon the pair were engaged in a frantic tug of war. Martin was by far the stronger and bigger of the two, but Billy refused to let go, no matter how hard Martin pulled. The idea of his friend falling into the hands of this bully was too much for him to bear. In desperation, Billy summoned all of his strength, and with a desperate shout of 'No!' he put all of his effort into one last pull, and snatched the lamp out of the surprised Martin's grasp. Caught quite off balance, Martin toppled into a nearby bin, eliciting laughs from the now very large crowd around them.

But Billy didn't hear anyone laughing. All he could hear was his own frightened breathing as he help the lamp so close to him that it hurt, so close that Marcel could probably hear his heart hammering away through the walls of his home. He didn't notice that the 8.25 was now in sight, and that the baying crowd had started to disperse, now more preoccupied with getting a seat for the journey into school. He didn't notice that Martin had risen to his feet, with blood under his nose from where his had fallen, and that he was looking at him with hatred. He didn't even notice as Martin strode towards him once more, and he only became aware of the outside world once more as he looked up and saw Martin standing in front of him. He looked more angry than Billy had ever seen anyone look, and before

Billy had time to think about anything else Martin gave him a hard shove in the chest, pushing him right off the edge of the platform and into the path of the oncoming train.

It was then that something very peculiar happened. As he fell Billy felt something strike him from behind, as if a great cushion of air had hit him head on, and he found himself twisting and falling back onto the platform. He looked up and saw that Martin must have tripped, although on what he had no idea, or perhaps been caught off balance by his own shove, for it was Martin who fell headlong right off the platform and under the 8.25.

And that was the end of Martin Proud.

School was cancelled that day. The next day Billy was called into the headmaster's office to give an account of what had happened. He wasn't in trouble, for everyone who had been there had already been questioned, and all agreed that it couldn't have been Billy's fault that Martin fell. The poor boy must have just lost his balance. The headmaster did ask to see this lamp that they had been fighting over, but Billy, sitting with it in his bag at his feet, told him that he had thrown it away.

He still carried the lamp around with him everywhere he went. No one teased him any more but he still liked to know that his friend was there with him, sitting in his bag with that little twinkly smile of his. The lamp wasn't nearly as shiny as it had been before, but of course Billy would never dream of polishing it. As he swung his bag, which felt lighter, as everything did these days, he smiled to think of what Marcel would say if he knew what had happened to Martin.

A whole week went by before Simon spoke to him about what had happened at the train station that day. They were sitting having lunch on their own in the corner of the playground, when Simon, who had clearly had something on his mind for quite some time, suddenly said,

'I'm sorry, you know, for not helping you more when Martin tried to take your pot from you.'

'It's a lamp,' said Billy, chewing his sandwich thoughtfully. 'There's not much you could have done, and it doesn't really matter now anyway.'

'How did you do it?' Simon asked. 'Fall like that, I mean. No one knows how you managed to end up back on the platform.'

'It was just luck, I suppose.' Billy shrugged.

'Did you do something with that lamp of yours?'

This time Billy looked up sharply.

'What do you mean?'

'It looked like you kind of jolted it in your hands or something when Martin pushed you. It was odd, but then I suppose you do odd things like that when you're scared, don't you?'

Billy stopped chewing. He suddenly felt sick.

'I jolted it?'

Without waiting for an answer Billy leapt to his feet and ran to the school nurse. He told her that he felt ill and need to go home immediately. Unsurprised, given recent events, she let him go, and he ran to the train station. That train journey home was the longest twenty minutes of Billy's life, and he sat impatiently as the train crawled home. The sick feeling in his stomach was growing and growing, and by the time the train lurched to a stop at his station Billy was beside himself. It was the middle of the afternoon, and everyone else was either at school or at work, and once the train had pulled away Billy found himself quite alone on the platform. He looked around him and found the bin that Martin had fallen into, and opposite, on the edge of the platform, where he had been standing when Martin pushed him. He fell to his knees and began to scrabble around in the dirt there, digging through the grime from the feet of hundreds of busy commuters. And it was there that he found it. It had been several days now since Martin had fallen, and it had been trampled into the dirt and the soot but it was still there; a single, golden star, the last star from Marcel's coat that had fallen when he'd left his lamp one final time to help his friend.

Her Master's Tree

In olden times when wishing still helped, a good, simple man called Alas, a potter by trade, was walking home one day when he came across a very sorry sight by the side of the road. It was an old man, and he had evidently been wandering for many days, quite lost and alone, for he was lying in a dead faint from hunger, with no companions around him. Noting with alarm that the chill of night would soon be upon them, Alas put the old man on his horse and took him home with him. When they got there he built up the biggest fire he could in the hearth and bade the stranger sit in front of it while he cooked him a heart warming dinner with what little food he had. Then, when he had made sure that the traveller had eaten his fill he gave him his own bed to sleep in, with plenty of blankets to keep the cold of the evening at bay, while he himself slept on the floor.

The old man was moved to tears by this kindness, and in the morning told Alas that he would like to reward him handsomely for what he had done for him. But Alas wouldn't take a thing, protesting that he hadn't done anything out of the ordinary. He could hardly have left the old man there to his death.

'Alas,' the old man said before he left, 'I owe you my life, and I'll never forget that. You have behaved better to me than my own sons would have, and you deserve every happiness and success in life. I hope we meet again, my friend.'

And so saying the old man took his leave. But the two never did meet again. As the years passed, Alas' business as a simple potter grew, and he did indeed become more successful, so much so that he found he needed to take on an apprentice to live with him, a young girl by the name of Aama, to keep up with the growing demand for his wares.

Aama, Alas soon found, was the perfect apprentice. She was hard working, attentive, and a quick learner. She was also extremely talented. Under Alas' expert guidance she became an excellent maker of pots. The two got on extremely well, and she quickly became like a daughter to Alas. She had been orphaned at a young age, and came to view him as the father she had never had.

Life was good for Alas and Aama. They were certainly very comfortable, but had never dreamt that they might ever be rich until one day an unusual looking man knocked on their door.

He was a messenger, he said, and he was the smartest looking man either Alas or Aama had ever seen. He was dressed in a bright blue suit with sparkling gold buttons and the shiniest of shoes. Over one shoulder he wore a deep red sash, and he had the manner of one who carried Messages of Importance.

His master, he explained to Alas, had until recently been the old man that Alas had helped all those years ago as he lay lost and hungry on the side of the road. Although Alas had refused to take any reward, his old master had never forgotten the kindness done to him. His old master had been rich, the messenger told him. He had three sons, but they were selfish and lazy, and his master had deemed them not worthy to inherit his fortune when he died (at this the messenger removed his cap and a look of sorrow passed over his face). Instead, he had left his entire fortune to Alas in gratitude for saving his life.

Alas could scarce believe his ears.

'A fortune?!' he repeated in excitement. Then, after thinking for a moment, he continued, almost apologetically, 'But forgive me, sir, I have never come across a fortune before. How much might a fortune be exactly?'

At this the messenger, in a show of impeccable good taste and discretion, took a very expensive looking pencil and sheet of the whitest paper from his pocket and wrote on it a number with more zeroes than any number has any right to have. He then handed the paper to Alas. Alas looked at the number in silent amazement, his eyes starting from his head as the messenger made ready to take his leave.

'I will be back shortly,' he explained, 'with my old master's will, to prove that what I've said is the truth, and that this fortune is indeed yours.'

At this Aama had to steady her master, so shocked and excited was he.

'What a day!' Alas cried, kissing the messenger, who nodded stiffly in return. 'Please, sir, you must stay and celebrate with us awhile before leaving, for you bring such happy news, we might do what we can to repay you.'

At this the messenger regretfully shook his head.

'I'm afraid I cannot,' he replied. 'I serve the sons of my old employer now. They are short tempered and cruel, and if I'm not back soon they will beat me.'

And so saying he bowed deeply to Alas and Aama, jumped on his horse and galloped away.

Immediately Alas told Aama to run to the nearest town and to but the fattest calf she could, and to invite everyone she met to a feast at his house that night.

'For tonight,' he said, 'we shall celebrate as never before! Good fortune like this deserves to be shared.'

And Alas was true to his word. That night he laid on a feast for his friends and neighbours the like of which no one had ever seen before. There was wine and dancing and laughter, and more food than a party of twice the size could possibly have eaten. People drank and ate and sang and danced late into the night, and it wasn't until the early hours of the morning that Alas finally got to bed, thinking himself the happiest, luckiest man in all the world.

But when Alas woke up later that day he was surprised to find himself not in his bed, nor even in his room. Instead, he was lying on a cold, stone floor in what looked very much to him like a prison cell, with a thick, locked door at one end. There was one window, and when Alas looked through the iron bars that covered it he saw with some alarm that he was high up, at the top of a tall tower, many miles away from home.

It was some hours before Alas had any further clues as to where he was and what had happened. The sun was beginning to set when he heard slow, heavy footsteps making their way up the tower. Hoping that they might be approaching him Alas listened intently, and the footsteps did indeed stop outside his door. He heard a key turn in the lock, and then the door flew open to reveal a huge, ugly man, holding a small plate of food and a cup of water.

'Ah, so you're awake, are you?' he said as he thrust the cup and the plate that held just a crust of bread and a couple of mouldy potatoes towards Alas.

'Who are you?' Alas asked in confusion, 'Where am I?'

'So you think you're going to take what's rightfully ours from my brothers and me, do you?' the big man replied, glowering down at Alas. 'Well, not any more you're not. You're staying here until we can think of what to do with you. I'll let you work out who we are yourself, and as to where you are,' at this the big man smiled cruelly, 'you're a very long way from home, little potter.'

With no more words he turned and left the room. Alas heard the door lock once more, and the big ugly footsteps descend, leaving him to his lonely meal in the rapidly darkening room.

The next day was the same. And the next, and the next. Alas would see or hear no one else apart from once a day when one of his captors would bring him some food and water. There were three of them, and they were all just as big and ugly as each other. They were half Alas' age and twice as big, and he knew better than to try to run when they brought him his food, for it would have been hopeless to try to get past such brutes. They never said more than a few words to him, and, apart from the brief conversation he had had on that first day of his imprisonment, he learnt nothing more about his situation.

As the long, lonely days turned into weeks, Alas slowly gave up any hope of seeing home again, and resigned himself to living in his cell for the rest of his days, or until the brothers thought of what to do with him, whichever came first. And so you can imagine his surprise when one night he heard a scrabbling sound just below his window, and suddenly a familiar face appeared at the bars.

'Master,' Aama whispered into the darkness. 'Master, are you there?'

In joy, Alas leapt to his feet and ran to the window.

'Oh yes!' he cried, shaking with happiness. 'Oh yes, Aama, I'm here. I'm being held captive by three brothers who think I've stolen a great fortune from them. Please, you must help me to escape!'

'I know it,' said Aama. 'They are the three brothers whose father's fortune you have inherited. They intend to keep you here until they think that the world has forgotten about you. Then they will do away with you and keep the fortune for themselves. Take this file,' she said, passing a small iron file through the bars to Alas, 'and file away at the bars, a little each day, so that the change isn't noticed. Weaken them, but don't break them. In a few weeks, when they are weak enough, I will return, and we will make good your escape.'

And as suddenly as the face had appeared it disappeared once more as Aama started the long climb back down the tower before daylight found her.

Alas did as his young apprentice had told him. Every day he would file away at the bars at his window, just a small amount each day, so that any change in appearance couldn't be noticed by someone who saw them almost every day as his captors did. Over the weeks they became so weak that Alas felt that he could easily snap them with his hands, but he did as he was told and waited for Aama to reappear.

And as she'd said she would, Aama did indeed reappear at his window one night many weeks later. She had with her a rope this time, and after easily snapping the weakened bars at the window they made good their escape by climbing down the tower to freedom. Once safely on the ground, Aama led them to an old barn where she had prepared a space under the floor where they could hide. Once they were safely settled into their temporary new home Aama explained to Alas what must be done.

'After the party,' she said, 'I woke up and the house was empty. You were nowhere to be found. I asked all of our friends and neighbours, but you weren't with any of them. I was beginning to give up hope when one day a very unexpected visitor knocked at the door.

It was the same messenger who had visited us to tell us about your inheritance! He told me everything; that you were being kept in that tower and what was to become of you. He also told me where the brothers lived.

They live in a big house not far from here. I follow them every day and listen to them, and know all of their plans, such as they are. They are incredibly stupid, and are constantly fighting amongst themselves, and they can never decide what to do. They want to destroy their father's will, but they don't know where it is, for he hid it from them, knowing what they were like. My guess is that it's hidden somewhere in the house, and if we can find it before they do we can claim what is rightfully yours!'

'But what about the messenger?' Alas asked. 'Surely he must know where this will is.'

At this Aama shook her head sadly, and took off her cap.

'He did know, and had promised to return with the will himself, but before he had a chance the brothers found out what he had told me. They slew him on the spot.'

'But we must act quickly,' Aama went on, drying her eyes. 'As soon as the brothers discover that you have escaped they will leave no stone unturned in hunting you. The only way you will be safe is if we find the will before they do.'

Although Alas protested that he should be the one do to it, it was decided in the end that Aama, the smaller and nimbler of the two, should be the one to search for the will. Every day master and apprentice lay low in their hiding place under the barn while the brothers scoured the surrounding country in search of them, and every night Aama would creep out from where she and her master lay and make her way to the brothers' house. There, while the inhabitants were sleeping, Aama, would go from room to room, as quiet as a mouse, looking for the piece of paper that would set her master free.

For three nights she undertook this dangerous task, and on the third night she found what she was looking for. Folded up carefully, behind a loose stone in the fireplace, was the old man's will, leaving his entire fortune to Alas. Hurriedly she stole away again into the night, bearing the precious piece of paper.

Aama and Alas lost no time. The very next day they went to the palace and begged an audience with the king on a matter, they said, of life and death. They were granted one, and, presenting the will, they explained all to their astonished monarch. The king was outraged. He summoned the three brothers to him immediately and banished them from him kingdom, telling them never to return. Alas was rewarded with what was rightly his, and overnight found himself a very rich man indeed.

But despite Alas' his new found wealth he didn't built himself a castle or a big manor house, but instead chose to stay in the simple home he had always lived in. And although he had no need to work ever again he asked Aama if she would continue living with him, to which she readily agreed.

And so for many long years Alas and Aama lived together in their home, looking after each other and never wanting for anything. Alas wasn't an acquisitive man, and he spent his fortune on gifts for his family and friends, and helping those in need. He was admired throughout the kingdom, and even the king himself said that he had never been so proud of any citizen as he was of the kind Alas.

As the years wore on Aama met a young man and fell in love. When they were married Alas was present as her father, a role he described as the proudest in all his life. He had a house built for them both next door to his, and the three lived very happily, side by side, well into Alas' old age.

But sadly all good things cannot last. One day, many years later, Alas, now an old man, was dozing in his front garden in the midday sun when a huge, bloodthirsty troll suddenly burst into view, ravenous for human flesh. It attacked Aama's house, smashing a hole in the roof with its huge fist and grabbing the unfortunate woman from inside. It hadn't had time to bring the struggling Aama to its open mouth, however, before Aama's husband came rushing out of the house with his sword. He bravely attacked the creature, but was swatted aside like an irritating fly.

By this time the commotion had woken the dozing Alas, and upon seeing the danger that Aama was in he jumped up as if he were a man thirty years younger and ran at the troll, picking up the first thing he could find from the rubble that littered the lawn, which was the small file that Aama had given him many years ago to file through the bars of his prison in the tower.

Feeling no fear, Alas ran at the troll and stabbed the file as deep as he could into its leg, cutting it slightly. In surprise, the troll dropped Aama, and turned to see who had dared to do such a thing. When he saw Alas standing there with the little file in his hand he picked him up with a roar of anger, intent on eating this impudent little man.

So preoccupied was the troll with this new quarry that it failed to notice Aama, who had risen and run to her dazed husband. She picked up his sword that lay alongside him and ran back to the troll. As the brute took the struggling Alas in both hands she drove the sword with all her might into its black heart.

With an almighty crash the troll fell to the ground, quite dead. Terrified, Aama ran to her former master, but it was too late; the troll had already crushed the life from his old body.

Distraught, Aama and her husband held the biggest funeral they could for Alas, and people came from far and wide to bid him farewell. He had touched so many with his kindness and generosity, and the king himself led the funeral procession of this kind, simple man. He had left everything he owned to Aama, and she rebuilt her house and lived in it just as before, using her fortune to help friends and neighbours all over the kingdom, just as Alas had done. And at the spot where he had died saving her life she planted a single acorn that has now grown into a magnificent oak tree. A stronger tree, it is said, has never stood. And I daresay it still stands there today.

The Man and the River

Once, many years ago, a man quarrelled with a river about who was the strongest.

'Look at my big, thick arms,' he said. 'I can fell trees and build walls, plough fields and dig wells. What can you do to match that?'

'I too can fell trees,' the river replied. 'and I can knock down your walls as easily as you can put them up. I can drown your fields and fill your wells, I could carry you out to sea as if you were a twig if I were so minded. Surely you can't think that you are stronger than me?'

'Let us wrestle,' suggested the man, 'and that will decide the matter.'

And so the two agreed to wrestle. They appointed a gorilla, who happened to be sitting on the riverbank watching this curious exchange, as referee, and the man stepped into the river and the contest began. The river withdrew a great distance upstream, and at a signal from the gorilla flung herself forward with all her might, roaring at the man for all she was worth.

The man was nearly knocked off his feet, but he held his ground. For his part though, he was unable to get a hold of the river to wrestle her as she rushed past him.

'Changeable river,' he said, 'you must change into something I can hold on to, for we cannot fight like this.'

And so the river withdrew once more and changed herself into a huge bull, charging fiercely at the man.

The man grabbed the bull by the horns and pulled it this way and that, but still neither of them were any closer to being knocked off their feet. And so the river changed herself into a gigantic serpent and wrapped herself around the man in an effort to squeeze him into submission, but the man wrapped his giant hands around the serpent's neck and squeezed back just as hard.

They fought like this for many days, with neither of them gaining the upper hand, until they were stopped by a small voice from the riverbank.

'Stop you two, look what you've done!'

They turned and saw a little mouse perched above them on a tree, pointing at the river's course with horror. They both turned and saw a dry riverbed all around them, full of dying fish, desperately thrashing about as they lay drowning in the mud. Homeless frogs and turtles and many other animals wandered aimlessly, having nowhere to live anymore. And the river looked further down her course and saw crops dying and villages with dry wells and nothing to drink. She was suddenly deeply ashamed, for she had abandoned her charge for the sake of vanity. She changed herself once more into a river, flowing freely again to fill her course and give life once more to the many animals and people that depend on her.

At this the gorilla declared that the man was the winner, for the river, in changing herself back to water, had been the first to touch the ground. The man cheered and leapt from the water, walking off in triumph back to his village, now rejoicing that its well had become full once more.

Rivers have never forgotten this betrayal, and ever since then have held a special hatred for gorillas, who above all other animals are the most afraid of running water. Nor have rivers forgiven the man's part in this, and from then on have never allowed themselves to be dammed or diverted or tamed by humans easily or meekly. They will flood their banks spitefully as they remember that contest, gleefully ruining peoples' homes, and will carry our boats only with the greatest of reluctance. No, nothing has such a memory as a river scorned, just as nothing has such arrogance as humans.

No More Room

At a time when rivers never ran dry and wishes could come true, a wandering prince came to an old castle in search of shelter for the night. He was greeted by the gatekeeper, who explained that although the old king who lived there was indisposed, he was welcome to stay with them, and that the servants would extend all possible hospitality they could towards him. The prince was delighted with this reception, and soon found himself very comfortably settled in a large room at the end of the east wing of the castle.

The next day he went out to explore the nearby countryside, for he had never been to this kingdom before. He was out all day, and night had fallen by the time he finally returned to the castle, where he was welcomed just as warmly as the day before, and given a wonderful dinner before he retired for the night.

When he got back to his room he felt that it was somehow smaller than it had been – it certainly didn't seem to be as spacious as he had supposed yesterday. He went to fetch an old book from one of his bags that a servant had put next to a wall when he had arrived, only to find that the bag was gone. This puzzled him greatly, and he went to sleep wondering what on earth could have happened to his things.

He slept very well, and the first thing he saw when he woke up was the bag in question against the wall, exactly where he thought it had been left. He went to breakfast more confused than ever, and he resolved to explore this mysterious castle where things seemed to disappear and reappear at random.

He spent the day exploring the gardens and thickets that surrounded the castle. It was high up on a hill, and whichever side of it the prince stood on he found that he could see far out over the surrounding land. When he reached the east wing he turned back to the castle to see if he could make out his bedroom window. He could indeed, and he was surprised to see that there was in fact a room next to his at the end of the wing, as he had thought that his room had been the last one. Not that that was of any consequence, he thought, and he spent the rest of the day comfortably resting in the castle grounds until his growling stomach commanded him to go back inside for dinner.

He ate splendidly again, and it was well after dark by the time he had finished his food and made for bed. When he got to the door of his room he tried the handle but was surprised to find that the door was locked. He tried again and thought that he heard a sharp intake of breath from within, followed by light feet running to the door. There was then an expectant silence, as if whoever was on the other side was waiting for something.

Confused, the prince stepped away from the door. He realised that he had walked straight past his room, and was in fact outside the room next door at the very end of the wing. Whoever was inside evidently didn't wish to be disturbed, and, calling an apology through the door, he carefully made his way back to his own room.

Once he was inside, it seemed somehow smaller again in the dark of the evening. Suddenly curious about his neighbour, the prince he leaned out of his window and looked to see if he could glimpse anything through the window next door. He couldn't see through the glass, but a light clearly shone out of it. Every now and then a shadow seemed to quickly flit past it, as if whoever was there was dancing or running around. The prince called to them, but there was no answer, and indeed, the window seemed to be closed.

The next morning over breakfast the prince asked a servant who might be staying in the room next to his. The servant looked at him in concern.

'Begging your pardon your lordship, but there isn't anyone staying in the room next to yours.'

'Nonsense!' answered the prince. 'I nearly walked in there by mistake last night, and would have disturbed whoever was in there if they hadn't locked the door.'

But the servant was insistent.

'Your lordship must be mistaken, I can assure you that there isn't anyone in the room you're talking about.'

More than a little put out by this the prince went straight back upstairs after breakfast. Deliberately this time, he walked straight past the door to his room, intending to try to get into the room next door. He was confounded, however, to find that the door to the room next door had been bricked up. Impossible! There had most definitely been a door there last night, but from the look of the stonework it looked like it had been blocked up many years ago. If you hadn't been looking closely you would have been forgiven for thinking that there hadn't been a door there at all, for only the faintest outline was still visible amongst the stones.

To say that the prince was now unsettled would be putting in mildly, and he hurried back to his room, which he was thankful to see looked much bigger in the daylight. He decided to leave the castle first thing in the morning, there was something unnatural about it, he thought, and he was beginning to mistrust his own eyes.

He spent the rest of the day far away from the castle, not wanting to be in the place for any longer than was necessary. That night over supper he asked a servant to pass on his apologies to the king, but he must leave with first light the next day. He ate barely anything, and went to bed early.

He was woken in the middle of the night by the unmistakable sound of someone dancing in the room next door. There was no doubt about it, and as the prince listened he marvelled that the steps hadn't woken the rest of the castle, they were so loud. He wasn't left to wonder this for long, however, for there was soon a knock at his door.

At the knock the sound of the dancing abruptly stopped, and the prince opened the door to reveal the same servant that he had spoken to at breakfast.

'I beg pardon, your lordship, but might I ask that you refrain from dancing like that in the middle of the night? You're waking the whole castle.'

The prince bade the servant come in, and replied that he hadn't been the one dancing, but the steps had come from the room next to his. The servant opened his mouth to reply, but before he could do so the dancing started again with renewed vigour. He looked at the wall and sat down dumbstruck on the bed.

'Come now,' said the prince, 'don't tell me you can't hear that! Yet this morning it looked to me as if that room had been blocked up. How do you explain that?'

The servant looked sick.

'Your lordship,' he said, 'many years ago the king had a daughter by the name of Heina. She was a beautiful thing, the apple of his eye, and we all loved her like she was our own. But alas, Heina came down with a fatal sickness before she was nine years old. She weakened so fast! The king was desperate, and consulted every doctor in the kingdom. They all told him the situation was hopeless and our king, overcome with grief and unable to watch his only daughter die, had the room bricked up while she slept in order to spare himself the pain of ever burying her. He has kept himself locked in his room ever since, refusing everything but food and drink.'

The prince jumped up.

'But we must let her out at once! King or no king, we can't keep the poor child bricked up in there for another moment!'

At this the servant looked quite ill.

'Sire, the room was sealed twenty years ago.'

Neither man noticed this time that the dancing had stopped again.

'This room we sit in now was extended into it five summers past,' the man continued. 'There is no room next to yours on that side any longer, nor has there been for some time.'

The prince felt a chill as he heard this, and he looked about the room, noticing that once again it seemed smaller. He felt the walls pressing in on him. He opened his mouth to reply, but this time it was his turn to be cut short as the dancing steps started once more, and the clear sound of a small girl singing rose above them. The servant turned pale, and they both rushed out into the corridor. Where the prince had seen a bricked up doorway that morning they now both saw a door, with light shining under it from the room within.

The prince, followed by the servant, went to the door and tried the handle, only to find that once again it was locked. The dancing and the singing both abruptly stopped. The men, standing outside the door, turned and looked at each other. As they did so the door opened slightly and a small girl's arm reached through and grabbed the servant by the shoulder. The terrified man was nearly pulled into the room, but without thinking the prince wrapped both arms around him and pulled him away from the pale arm's grip. It quickly withdrew back into the room, and the door shut again. Without thinking, the prince grabbed the door handle and turned it, but it wouldn't open.

The petrified servant fled, leaving the prince standing alone facing the door. He stood there for some minutes, wondering what to do. He was on the verge of running away himself when the servant returned with another man. They carried with them a ladder of stout oak.

Without a word passing between them the prince, scared as he was, took the ladder with them. All three men then ran at the door with all their might, using the ladder as a battering ram. Once, twice, three times they ran at the door, but it wouldn't budge. They gathered themselves for one final effort and ran full pelt at the door, only to be knocked to the floor as the ladder splintered and gave way, for they had run against a solid stone wall. It was now dawn, and the door had disappeared.

True to his word, the prince left that morning, riding from the castle as soon as he was able. Tarrying as he left, he turned to take one last look at the place, gazing up at his window and seeing, once again, the princess' window next to his. He was about to leave when he saw something lying at the foot of the castle under the last window, as if it had been knocked carelessly from its sill. He went to it and picked it up. It was a small rag doll, the sort that a girl of about nine years old might have played with when no one would come and visit her any more.

The prince went on to have many adventures over the years to come, and fight bravely in a great many battles. He saw more of the world than most of us, but he would always say that nothing he had faced had saddened him so much as the lost princess in that castle.

Where Thorn Bushes Come From

Far away, at the edge of the world, on the top of a very steep hill, there once lived a spiteful old farmer who cared for no one, and he especially hated witches. It was unfortunate for him then that a witch just so happened to live in a small hut on his land with her daughter, not far from his own house. She was a very kind, proper sort of a witch who never used her powers to harm people, but the farmer hated her nonetheless, and would take every opportunity he could to make her life a misery. He would always speak unkindly to her, and never help her to gather in wood in the chill of winter, or give her food when he had spare. He made a habit of ignoring her when he passed her in the lane, and would tell everyone he met terrible lies about her.

One day he killed her cat, for he said that it had stolen his cream. This was of course a lie, and the witch knew it. She'd been extremely fond of her cat, and was tremendously sad at its loss. However, she held her tongue, not wanting to fight with her neighbour. Her daughter, though, had other ideas.

'Let's chop off his feet!' she cried. 'Let's tear out his tongue! Let's set a pack of wolves on him and see him eaten alive!'

But the witch would allow her daughter to do no such thing.

'Two wrongs will never make a right,' she cautioned her child. 'We shouldn't use our powers to bring harm, only good. He'll see the error of his ways. Do as I say and leave him be.'

And so the hot headed girl stayed her hand at her mother's insistence, and both hoped that that would be an end to the matter.

Sadly, it wasn't. A few weeks later, when the witch thought that perhaps the farmer had grown out of his spite, he took her broomstick from her front porch. When she noticed that it had gone the next day and asked him about it he replied that he had needed firewood, and had broken it up and burnt it. Now, a witch's broomstick is more dear to her than anything else, and the witch was devastated. Still she didn't say a word of reproach, for she didn't want to start a rift with her landlord. Once again though, her daughter was of a different mind.

'We must curse him!' She cried. 'Turn him into a bear! A toad! Put a toad on his face! We must be revenged, mother.'

But still the witch cautioned restrained.

'We are the ones with powers,' she said, 'not he. We should use them for good, not vengeance.'

But this course of inaction did her no good. Some weeks later the farmer saw fit to throw her and her daughter out of their house, claiming that they were a nuisance. The witch certainly knew that this was a lie, for they had never done anything to wrong the farmer, and she told him so.

'I don't care,' he said. 'I know your type. It's only a matter of time before you do something. You witches are no good, I know that much. Begone from my land, I've put up with you for far too long!'

The witch protested, finally finding her voice, but it was too late, and the farmer wouldn't relent. And so the witch and her daughter had to leave their home. They left calling down curses on the farmer who simply laughed at them, and so that night they determined to get their revenge.

They waited until darkness had fallen and silently crept into the farmer's house and into his bedroom where he lay asleep. There, as he dreamed peacefully, the witch transformed his ears into those of a donkey as punishment for his crimes. But he looked so silly lying there with big long donkey ears sticking out from under his hair that her daughter couldn't help laughing at the sight of him. This woke the farmer up, and he sat up immediately when he saw the witches in his room. Then he caught sight of himself in the mirror, and knew what they had done.

In a rage he jumped out of bed and chased them both out of the house. He chased them across the fields and down the hill, shouting in fury all the time. He was a big man, and a much faster runner than them both, and the witch knew that soon he would catch them both. Terrified at what he might do to her daughter, she transformed herself into a thick bush with long, cruel thorns on it. The farmer, unable to stop, ran pell mell into the bush and found himself caught. He was trapped – the more he struggled the more the spikes tore at him, and he eventually died, stabbed all over from a million tiny thorns.

It is the descendants of this witch that are the thorn bushes that we see today. And the farmer has left his mark as well, for the berries that we see on thorn bushes nowadays are what remain of the drops of the farmer's blood that was first spilt on her thorns.

All comments welcome at alexbuxton2812@gmail.com

Printed in Great Britain
by Amazon